Samuel French Acting Edition

Splitting Heirs

by Freyda Thomas

Inspired by
Regnard's *Le Légataire universel*

SAMUELFRENCH.COM   SAMUELFRENCH.CO.UK

FOR PRODUCTION ENQUIRIES

UNITED STATES AND CANADA
Info@SamuelFrench.com
1-866-598-8449

UNITED KINGDOM AND EUROPE
Plays@SamuelFrench.co.uk
020-7255-4302

Each title is subject to availability from Samuel French, depending upon country of performance. Please be aware that *SPLITTING HEIRS* may not be licensed by Samuel French in your territory. Professional and amateur producers should contact the nearest Samuel French office or licensing partner to verify availability.

MUSIC USE NOTE

Licensees are solely responsible for obtaining formal written permission from copyright owners to use copyrighted music in the performance of this play and are strongly cautioned to do so. If no such permission is obtained by the licensee, then the licensee must use only original music that the licensee owns and controls. Licensees are solely responsible and liable for all music clearances and shall indemnify the copyright owners of the play(s) and their licensing agent, Samuel French, against any costs, expenses, losses and liabilities arising from the use of music by licensees. Please contact the appropriate music licensing authority in your territory for the rights to any incidental music.

IMPORTANT BILLING AND CREDIT REQUIREMENTS

If you have obtained performance rights to this title, please refer to your licensing agreement for important billing and credit requirements.

CHARACTERS

ERASTE – Nephew to Geronte, bumbling, awkward, shy, loveable, scared of his uncle, madly in love with:

ISABELLE – The girl next door. Everything you've ever wanted in an ingénue and less. Never says more than three words in a row until the epilogue. Conveys her character in poses. Lisps.

CRISPIN – (Pronounced Kree-SPAN.) Servant to Eraste, jack-of-all-trades, bon vivant, master of disguise. Fences, plays a German doctor, a woman, and impersonates Geronte.

LISETTE – Prototype comic maid, servant to Geronte, in love with Crispin. Sharp, sassy, plays a man in one scene.

GERONTE – An old, sick miser. Dies several times.

MME ARGANTE – Isabelle's mother. Lady Bracknell in Paris.

POQUELIN – Geronte's lawyer. A very short man. (Also plays the Gendarme's assistant.)

PIERRE – Poquelin's assistant, also the Gendarme.

PROLOGUE

(The stage is black except for a special on **ISABELLE** *and* **ERASTE**. *He is on one knee. She faces away from him, frozen in a lovely, demure tableau. He hesitates, then speaks. She moves only to change poses.)*

ERASTE.

My dearest Isabelle – I – that is –

ISABELLE.

Yes?

ERASTE.

I have a secret longing to confess.
One which I carry with me in my heart.
May I impart its thought to you?

ISABELLE.

Impart.

ERASTE.

(During his next lines he prompts himself from crib sheets fastened to various parts of his body – inside his hat, coat, on the sole of his shoe, etc.)

Well, then, dear Isabelle, I mean – uh –

ISABELLE.

Yes?

ERASTE.

If but my heart could speak, it would confess
A hundred sweet enchantments which your face
Creates within it. Let me words embrace
Your –

ISABELLE.

Oh!

ERASTE.

Heart, as yours has embraced my own,
Which beats, here, evermore, for you alone.
The moment we first met – when?

ISABELLE.

Yesterday.

ERASTE.

I felt a peace surround my sorry way.
Since first I heard the music in your voice –

ISABELLE.

(Demonstrating.)

Ah! Ah!

ERASTE.

That makes the wingéd bird rejoice.
Would I could better fashion into speech
The love I bear you. How must I beseech,
Explain, cajole and flatter such a sense
That you might not show cool indifference
To this sweet longing that my soul endures
In its desire to be as one with yours.
It wanders, silent, lonely, late at night,
In search of an oasis of requite
For its most tender passion –

ISABELLE.

Oh!

ERASTE.

Forgive
The candor of my ardor, but to live
In doubt and darkness, aching so to pass
Into the light of your sweet eyes –

ISABELLE.

Alas!

ERASTE.

Tell me your loving heart desires to cure
This tender malady, so clear, so pure –

ISABELLE.

Yes!

ERASTE.

Then, do you consent to let me dwell
In paradise with dearest Isabelle?
Your honeyed lips need only to confess
That you might condescend to love me –

ISABELLE.

Yes!

(Stunned that she has agreed, he collects himself, kisses her hand, and faints dead away. She turns and smiles down at him as the lights go to black.)

ACT I

Scene One

(A unit set. There is a balcony at the top of a flight of stairs having at least two doors leading onto it. There are three downstairs doors – the front door, one leading to the servants' quarters and kitchen, and one leading to the study, a room off the main room, which cannot be seen by the audience. At curtain rise **CRISPIN** *and* **LISETTE** *enter from opposite doors – she from upstairs, carrying a basin and a towel, he from the servants' quarters with a tray of paté. They pass each other formally and quickly, with a nod, get to their exit doors, stop, look around, back up slowly to each other, put down their props, and embrace passionately. Afterwards,* **CRISPIN** *points to the upstairs.)*

CRISPIN.

How is he?

LISETTE.

Terrible.

CRISPIN.

What – not again?

LISETTE.

And every day this week.

CRISPIN.

Mon Dieu.

LISETTE.

Amen.

It always starts the same way – "Aargh! I'm dying!"

The legs and arms go –

    (She demonstrates, sitting on the sofa.)

                It's terrifying.

His face turns blue, he clutches at his heart,
Falls lifeless on the pillow. "I depart,"
He rattles, eyes roll back into his head,
I cover him and pray, "Thank God he's dead,"
Walk to the door, convinced, I must admit,
He's gone. Then from the bed I hear, "You twit!
Come here!" I swear that man just loves to die.

CRISPIN.

Day after day we watch him calcify.

LISETTE.

I watch him. All you ever have to do
Is cater to that witless nephew.

CRISPIN.

                         True.

LISETTE.

I bathe him, feed him, humor him, comply
With every wheezing order –

CRISPIN.

                    I could cry.

LISETTE.

Each vile command allowed a dying man.

CRISPIN.

I sympathize.

LISETTE.

Imagine, if you can…

    (She imitates his voice.)

"It's time to let my blood! I want my shawl!"
At any hour of the day, that call –
"Lisette!" I change his linens, give him pills,
Cool down his fevers, elevate his chills,

Transport him to the wheelchair on my back,
Revive him after every new attack –
The poultices, cathartic and emetic –
The vile medications –

CRISPIN.

It's pathetic.

LISETTE.

(As he begins wooing her.)

Crispin...

CRISPIN.

(Murmuring in her ear.)

Lisette...

LISETTE.

My bear...

CRISPIN.

My pet...

LISETTE.

Stop that!

CRISPIN.

I love her when she's angry –

LISETTE.

We must chat.

CRISPIN.

All right, my little puma.

LISETTE.

(Extricating herself from his embrace.)

You sit here.

(She sits in a different chair.)

That's right. Now, angel, think back to last year.

CRISPIN.

Last year.

LISETTE.

That's right. Last May. A starry night.

No moon, a breeze, the stars were very bright.

CRISPIN.

Bright.

LISETTE.

Right. You spoke of us. That is to say,
Of you and me.

CRISPIN.

Oh, that us.

LISETTE.

Ah, touché.

Well, then?

CRISPIN.

Well, then?

LISETTE.

Well, when?

CRISPIN.

Well when? When what?

LISETTE.

When are we getting married?

CRISPIN.

Married?! But –

LISETTE.

But what? You love me?

CRISPIN.

Yes!

LISETTE.

Then marry me!

CRISPIN.

(Groping for an answer.)

As soon as I have an…annuity.

LISETTE.

Another foul disease!

CRISPIN.

No, no, a trust!

LISETTE.

You need a truss?

CRISPIN.

That's right. It's only just
So I may take good care of you, my dear.

LISETTE.

The old man's got a truss! I'll bring it here!

(She starts to go, he stops her.)

CRISPIN.

No, no, my swan!

(Aside.)

She's so adorable.

A TRUST of money.

LISETTE.

Oh.

CRISPIN.

A plentiful
Supply of cash in hand that will allow
Our comfort.

LISETTE.

Oh. How will you get it?

CRISPIN.

How.

(Making it up as he goes.)

A plan. So pure, so brilliant, so exquisite
In its simplicity, you'll say –

LISETTE.

What is it?

CRISPIN.

I don't know yet

LISETTE.

You don't know yet.

CRISPIN.

Just so.

LISETTE.

You will tell me the moment that you know.

(They sit and begin snacking on the paté.)

CRISPIN.

Of course.

LISETTE.

(Getting an idea.)

Of course…

CRISPIN.

Of course?

LISETTE.

If the old bird…

CRISPIN.

Geronte?

LISETTE.

Who else? Relented, and conferred

His fortune on Eraste –

CRISPIN.

His nephew?!

LISETTE.

Yes.

By your manipulation, I would guess
Eraste could be persuaded to endow…

CRISPIN.

A brilliant scheme!

LISETTE.

I know.

CRISPIN.

But how?

LISETTE.

                    Yes, how?

To get Geronte to leave that simpleton

A single sou –

CRISPIN.

                    The challenge could be fun.

First, let us both review the situation.

LISETTE.

My master hates your master.

CRISPIN.

                         Complication.

LISETTE.

Why does he hate him?

CRISPIN.

                    Simple. He was born.

His brother's only child. Geronte has sworn

To never pardon or forgive the deed.

LISETTE.

The deed.

CRISPIN.

        A shame, the way they disagreed.

Such hopes for brother dear the old man had.

A lawyer in the family –

LISETTE.

                    Too bad.

CRISPIN.

His life arranged for him. Except one factor.

The upstart runs away…to be an actor!

LISETTE.

No!

CRISPIN.

        Yes. They tell me all of France could see

The old man's face. As red as it could be

When he had read the note. "I've gone away

To find my true vocation" –

LISETTE.

Lackaday.

CRISPIN.

He choked, he gasped, he hopped around a bit,
And then he had an apoplectic fit!
Geronte was in a sorry state. At last
He managed to survive. The crisis passed,
But for the next four years his brother's name
Was never even whispered!

LISETTE.

Till *he* came.

CRISPIN.

Just popped down from the sky it seemed – voilà.
A baby boy. His brother's last faux pas
Before he passed away.

LISETTE.

Poor little thing.

CRISPIN.

Just sitting on that trunk and blubbering...

LISETTE.

The trunk! The one the old man likes to kick!
The very mention of it makes him sick.
So that's where all the costumes came from.

CRISPIN.

Yes.

The last remains of brother.

LISETTE.

Quelle tristesse.

Did brother...marry?

CRISPIN.

Yes! A costumière.

They met on his first tour with Molière.

LISETTE.

(They both cross themselves.)

Molière! That's quite a story.

CRISPIN.

            My soul weeps

To think of it.

LISETTE.

            And so the old man keeps

The boy, to punish him for Papa's crime.

CRISPIN.

Someday he'll pardon poor Eraste.

LISETTE.

               Meantime,

The task at hand.

CRISPIN.

               Eraste.

And the old man.

To cause a rapprochement we need a plan.

A delicate maneuvering, this task.

My master is too –

LISETTE.

        Ignorant –

CRISPIN.

        To ask

His uncle for a farthing. He's so good,

He only wants the old man's love. He would

Be genuinely crushed to see him die,

Yet stands to gain a fortune by it.

LISETTE.

        Why?

CRISPIN.

Upon the sad demise Eraste might be

The sole residuary legatee.

LISETTE.

The what?

CRISPIN.

The legal heir.

LISETTE.

There are no others?

CRISPIN.

There may be one or two.

LISETTE.

No sisters? Brothers?

Nieces?

CRISPIN.

Just Eraste and one or two

Relations – distant – from the country, who

Have never seen the old man.

LISETTE.

What a plot!

So then, is he the legal heir or not?

CRISPIN.

It all depends upon the will.

LISETTE.

The will.

CRISPIN.

My master cannot know his fate until

Your master draws a legal document

Deciding how and where the money's spent.

LISETTE.

Don't mention money!

CRISPIN.

No?

LISETTE.

It makes him cringe. He

Hates to spend a sou.

CRISPIN.

But why?

LISETTE.

He's stingy.

You want to know how cheap?

CRISPIN.

Not really, no.

LISETTE.

He pays me nothing.

CRISPIN.

(Falling to his knees and taking her hand.)

Why, the so and so!

I'd no idea! But why do you stay?

LISETTE.

(Aside.)

I stay because of him, but dare not say.
I must remain aloof. Can't let him know
How much I love my braggadocio!

(To him.)

Two reasons: First, at least it's a position.
Good food, a pleasant room, and in addition,
He lets me say whatever I'm inclined to.
I call him crocodile if I've a mind to.
Talk back and yell as often as I care.

CRISPIN.

He doesn't fire you?

LISETTE.

He wouldn't dare.

No other servant would agree to do
The terrible ordeals he puts me through.

CRISPIN.

(Getting amorous again.)

Your craft. Such expertise. I am impressed.

LISETTE.

My duck...

CRISPIN.

My goose...

LISETTE.

(Extricating herself again.)

I have to get him dressed.

Besides, we were discussing strategy.

CRISPIN.

Eraste. And how to make him legatee.

LISETTE.

Where is the witless wonder?

CRISPIN.

He's gone out.

He wouldn't tell me what it was about,

But he was in a state I've never seen!

His hands were trembling, and his face was green.

His usual incompetence was worse

Than ever. Several times I heard him curse!

He had his shoes on backwards, ripped a glove –

LISETTE.

Green face, ripped glove, shoes backwards? He's in love.

CRISPIN.

How do you know?

LISETTE.

It's obvious! But who?

CRISPIN.

Whom does he love? I haven't got a clue.

LISETTE.

Well, someone is the object of his dreams.

CRISPIN.

The boy has got some talent, so it seems.
You know, he's not as witless as one might
Be led to think. He's often almost bright.
It's old Geronte who makes him ill at ease.
Eraste will venture anything to please
The devil. Never works, of course. But mark
My words, that lad has got a certain spark.
A dormant courage, waiting to attack.
He may surprise us all one day –

ERASTE.

(Bursting in and surprising them.)

I'm back!

*(**LISETTE** screams and startles **ERASTE**, who steps in the enema pan, trips, and falls. He grabs the hot iron to steady himself, burns his hand, and then sticks it in the enema pan to cool it. General chaos.)*

CRISPIN.

*(To **LISETTE**.)*

You see? I told you.

*(To **ERASTE**.)*

Well? Where have you been?

ERASTE.

I've been to heaven!

CRISPIN.

And they let you in?
Sit down and tell me all about it.

ERASTE.

(Sitting, then standing.)

Well,
I went up to the door and rang the bell –

CRISPIN.

What bell?

ERASTE.

The doorbell.

CRISPIN.

(Aside.)

Patience.

(To him.)

Tell me more.

ERASTE.

I waited...

CRISPIN.

And?

ERASTE.

She opened up the door!

CRISPIN.

(To **LISETTE.***)*

She did?

LISETTE.

Imagine that!

CRISPIN.

Then what occurred?

ERASTE.

She said, "Come in." At first my mind was blurred,

(Gathering confidence, acting it out as he goes.)

But soon my voice returned. I said, "Merci."
She led the way. So very close were we,
That leaning forward, I could touch her hair!
I tripped, just once, upon a little chair.
We sat in the salon, the door was closed...
She smiled at me.

(He drifts into a reverie.)

CRISPIN & LISETTE.

And?

ERASTE.

Oh. Then I proposed.

LISETTE.

He did?

CRISPIN.

You did?

ERASTE.

I did.

CRISPIN.

I cannot wait

To hear the rest. Did she reciprocate
Your love?

ERASTE.

Reciprocate means to agree?

CRISPIN.

(Aside.)

Bright boy.

(He nods to **ERASTE.***)*

ERASTE.

Then she reciprocated me!

(A moment of joyous celebration for all, then **LISETTE** *stops the action.)*

LISETTE.

Who?

ERASTE.

Who?

CRISPIN.

Who?

LISETTE.

Who reciprocated you?

ERASTE.

Oh! Isabelle.

LISETTE.

Ah, Isabelle.

CRISPIN.

That's who.

Isabelle who?

ERASTE.

Next door.

CRISPIN.

A happy chance
To find so close at hand la belle romance.

ERASTE.

The brightest dearest angel –

LISETTE.

Say no more.

I'd rather hear the part about the door.

(Aside to **CRISPIN.***)*

And she returns his love!

CRISPIN.

Apparently.

LISETTE.

Quel plot.

ERASTE.

She has agreed to marry me!

CRISPIN.

What news! Felicitations! Uncle knows,
Of course.

ERASTE.

(Reality descends.)

Oh. Do you think he might oppose
Our union?

(He starts to pace.)

CRISPIN.

Ah, reality descends.

He starts to pace, he sits, he comprehends.

ERASTE.

Crispin! What shall I do? He must agree!

CRISPIN.

Of course he will. Leave everything to me.

ERASTE.

Oh good.

(He exits, returns immediately.)

What will we do?

CRISPIN.

No apprehension.

A simple, quick maneuver. Pay attention!

You bring her here to meet him.

ERASTE.

Ah!

(He exits, returns immediately.)

You're sure?

CRISPIN.

Do you have any doubt I shall procure

A happy ending for us all?

ERASTE.

Oh, no!

I trust your every word.

CRISPIN.

You should. Now, go!

*(He finally leaves. **CRISPIN** and **LISETTE** embrace.)*

If I get her for him, his joyous mood

Will be but shadows to his gratitude.

His nature, generous, unbridled, free,

Would guarantee a small annuity…
Let us conjecture – three?

LISETTE.

Eight.

CRISPIN.

                              Hundred francs
A year would fill my heart with…heartfelt thanks.
He went to get the bride – you get the man,
While I explain how all of this began!

> *(During the next monologue by* **CRISPIN**, **LISETTE**
> *brings a wheelchair into the main room from the
> study. She then goes upstairs to the old man's room
> and emerges with him on her back, carries him
> downstairs, and deposits him in the wheelchair,
> settles him in, puts his shawl around him.* **CRISPIN**
> *never turns around or offers a hand. At the end of
> his monologue the old man speaks.)*

A servant's life is not an easy one.
But then again, whose life is naught but fun?
Who does not sometime, somewhere in one's life
Experience a small degree of strife?
And though I may have more than others felt
The gnaw of hunger tight'ning at my belt,
Or once and frequently been forced to greet
The frosty nip of winter at my feet,
The chilblains in my joints from chopping wood,
In general, my life's been rather good!
A servant's life may have its ups and downs,
But truly, do the heads that wear the crowns
Lie easier than ours? I say nay, nay.
A servant's life may not be distingué,
And emptying of chamber pots may not
Be your idea of a grand gavotte,
Or climbing stairs or weeding gardens or

The washing and a hundred errands more,
But I'm not wont to dwell in dark despair,
For in here is much better than out there,
And wishing one were elsewhere than where one
Has found oneself to be is best not done.
So, though the concept seems a bit demented
And seeped in optimism, I'm contented!
Lament? Complain? Bemoan? Why, what's the good?
I'd not trade places with them if I could.
You think they're any happier than we?
Just watch how things progress and you will see.

GERONTE.

(By now **GERONTE** *is settled in. He barks.)*

What day is it?!

LISETTE.

(Also barking.)

It's Thursday.

GERONTE.

What's the date?

LISETTE.

The twelfth of May.

GERONTE.

What drops do I await?

LISETTE.

The green ones. Three o'clock.

GERONTE.

I need a nap.

(He falls asleep, wakes up.)

Lisette!

LISETTE.

What?!

GERONTE.

Where's my shawl?!

LISETTE.

It's in your lap!

(She throws it over his head. He speaks from beneath it.)

GERONTE.

Someday you'll go too far!

LISETTE.

Indeed I may!

GERONTE.

You twit!

LISETTE.

You yell at everything I say!

GERONTE.

Is this a way to treat a man who's ill?

LISETTE.

It's almost two o'clock. Here, take a pill.

(She opens his mouth, drops the pill in, closes his mouth, and slaps him on the back, as though she's done it a hundred times.)

Works every time.

CRISPIN.

A dandy system.

GERONTE.

Aahh.

(When he recovers.)

You wench!

LISETTE.

Decrepit coot!

GERONTE.

You're fired!

LISETTE.

Ha!

GERONTE.

Go pack! I'm throwing you into the street.

LISETTE.

Good. After this the street will be a treat.

GERONTE.

Now take me to the study.

LISETTE.

Certainly.

(She begins to wheel him in as they do the next exchange.)

GERONTE.

This heartless wench will be the death of me.
Lisette!

LISETTE.

What now!

GERONTE.

It's time for my emetic!

LISETTE.

You just had one.

GERONTE.

Well then, my diuretic.

LISETTE.

You had that too.

GERONTE.

I need a cataplasm.

LISETTE.

Oh, no you don't.

GERONTE.

I do! I'll have a spasm!

LISETTE.

Go right ahead.

GERONTE.

You lizard!

LISETTE.

Don't be glum.

In just a while it's time for laudanum.

GERONTE.

What time was my last...

(*Whispering to her.*)

LISETTE.

What?!

GERONTE.

My...you-know...

LISETTE.

Oh.

Now let me see...it's not yet time to go.

GERONTE.

Then leave me, crocodile!

LISETTE.

Avec plaisir.

GERONTE.

Don't show your face to me again!

LISETTE.

I cheer

To hear the welcome news, you clod!

GERONTE.

You scullion!

LISETTE.

Cur!

GERONTE.

Rag-picker!

LISETTE.

Scrub!

GERONTE.

Slubberdegullion!

LISETTE.

(She slams the study door, turns, and addresses **CRISPIN**.*)*

Now where were we? Oh, yes. The subject of
Our marriage. The annuity.

CRISPIN.

(Getting amorous again.)

And love.

LISETTE.

The task at hand.

CRISPIN.

The old man...

LISETTE.

How to broach

The subject of Eraste –

CRISPIN.

(Still making out.)

A soft approach.

LISETTE.

Do not rely on his senility.
The very mention of Eraste and he
Becomes a lucid man of thirty-five.
His venom is what keeps that man alive.
I've seen him go from stupor to irate
In seconds, if he's forced to contemplate
The subject of Eraste.

CRISPIN.

Leave him to me.

I'll use my talents in diplomacy.

LISETTE.

Diplomacy! Where did you learn?

CRISPIN.

I once

Apprenticed to a diplomat. A dunce
Who wanted me to write his oratory.
That night he spoke…but that's another story.
Now go and get him. No point in delaying
The scene.

(She goes to leave, he kisses her again.)

LISETTE.

(Aside, as she leaves.)

That man can kiss.

CRISPIN.

What was I saying?
Oh yes. Geronte. A case in point, poor soul.
Among the wealthy, life can take its toll,
And all his fortune cannot buy him youth
Or health, or love, or friends, and that's the truth.

LISETTE.

*(Wheeling **GERONTE** back in.)*

Well, here we are!

CRISPIN.

He looks so well today.
His skin's a rather piquant shade of gray.
Is he all right?

LISETTE.

Of course. He's in a trance.
Just mention – you-know-who.

CRISPIN.

All right.

LISETTE.

Bonne chance.

CRISPIN.

Your nephew, sir –

GERONTE.

(Waking instantly.)

That pea-brain? Say no more.

CRISPIN.

Sends greetings, and he hopes you won't deplore
His most sincere regard for your well-being.

GERONTE.

I'll bet he does.

CRISPIN.

If you'd agree to seeing
Him for just a moment –

GERONTE.

No!

LISETTE.

Be nice!

CRISPIN.

He's anxious to solicit your advice
About a somewhat delicate affair.

GERONTE.

That birdbrain's always getting in my hair!
All right. Where is he?

CRISPIN.

(Aside to **LISETTE.***)*

On his way, I hope.

(To **ERASTE.***)*

He's not quite here yet.

GERONTE.

Not here yet? The dope!

He wants to see me and he isn't here.
You are expecting him sometime this year?

CRISPIN.

(Looking out the window.)

Oh, yes indeed, I venture to presume
That shortly he'll be standing in this room.

> *(The door bursts open; it is* **ERASTE**. *The exuberance with which he opens the door causes an alabaster vase on a table by the door to fall and break. A silence.* **ERASTE** *is frozen in fear.)*

GERONTE.

Which priceless piece of pottery was that?

LISETTE.

The alabaster vase by Montserrat.

GERONTE.

The Montserrat?!

LISETTE.

Yes.

GERONTE.

Idiotic pup!

He'll never learn. Lisette!

LISETTE.

What!

GERONTE.

Clean it up!

ERASTE.

Oh uncle, I'm so sorry, please forgive
My clumsiness!

GERONTE.

And I am forced to live
In constant peril for my life – watch out!

> *(***ERASTE** *trips again over a piece of furniture.)*

ERASTE.

Oh, yes! Excuse me.

GERONTE.

Worthless knockabout.

I wonder that I'm still alive with him

Around me.

LISETTE.

(Aside to **CRISPIN.***)*

Things are looking somewhat grim.

ERASTE.

(Aside to **CRISPIN.***)*

Crispin!

CRISPIN.

(Edging to him.)

What is it?

ERASTE.

I have brought her.

CRISPIN.

Good.

Where is she?

ERASTE.

(Pointing out the door.)

There.

CRISPIN.

(Looking.)

Please tell me, if you would,

Who is that woman with her?

ERASTE.

Her mamá.

She wants to meet my uncle.

CRISPIN.

Oh, la la.

(Aside to **LISETTE**.*)*

CRISPIN.

He's sprung a mother on me.

LISETTE.

Oh what fun.

Another challenge!

CRISPIN.

Be prepared to run.

(They nod to each other. He goes to **GERONTE**.*)*

Oh sir! A grand occasion it would seem!
Your neighbors hold you in such high esteem
That they have ventured to our door to pay
Their great respects in person, here today.

GERONTE.

They never came before.

CRISPIN.

They've just moved in.

(Aside.)

Now let me see...the best place to begin...

(Aside to **ERASTE**, *after a quick reflection.)*

I'm ready. You may bring them in.

ERASTE.

Oh joy!

I knew you'd do it!

CRISPIN.

Try not to destroy

Another vase.

*(***ERASTE*** gets the ladies, **CRISPIN** speaks to
GERONTE.)*

May I present to you...

(A quick whispered conference with **ERASTE**.*)*

Madame Argante.

MME ARGANTE.

Delighted.

GERONTE.

How'd'ye do?

CRISPIN.

Her daughter Isabelle.

GERONTE.

Who? Isabelle?

LISETTE.

Yes!

ISABELLE.

How'd'ye do, sir.

GERONTE.

Who's this mademoiselle?

What is she doing here?

ERASTE.

(Aside to **CRISPIN.***)*

What do I say?

CRISPIN.

First offer them a chair.

ERASTE.

Oh, straightaway!

*(A great deal of confusion producing chairs for both
ladies.* **ERASTE** *trips and bumps into everyone.)*

GERONTE.

Excuse me for a moment. Psst, Lisette!

LISETTE.

Pardonnez-moi.

(She goes to **GERONTE.***)*

What is it?

GERONTE.

I forget…

What time…the diuretic…

LISETTE.

Ten past two.

It's not time yet.

GERONTE.

But soon! I'll signal you.

(They do an elaborate mime routine of exchanging signals, then return to the guests. LISETTE serves them the pâté. A moment of silence, which CRISPIN breaks.)

CRISPIN.

Madame? You've moved here?

MME ARGANTE.

Yes, from Compiegne. [com-pee-YEN]

LISETTE.

(After there is no reaction from GERONTE, shouting in his ear.)

They've moved from Compiegne!

GERONTE.

How's that again?

LISETTE.

I said Compiegne, you toad!

GERONTE.

I heard!

CRISPIN.

That's nice.

It's...nice in Compiegne.

MME ARGANTE.

One pays a price

For rustic life.

GERONTE.

A price? What price?

MME ARGANTE.

Good sir,

My daughter's future. I would not deter
The opportunity for wealthy suitors.
She's educated. Why, the finest tutors
Have shaped her character, refined her sense
And formed her spirit. I've spared no expense
Preparing her to take her place among
Her worthy peers. And though she is still young,
She's of a very marriageable age.

ERASTE.

She's very healthy –

(They both bring her forward to **GERONTE***.)*

CRISPIN.

Wiser than a sage –

(She produces a book from a basket she is carrying.)

ERASTE.

Her teeth are good...

(She smiles. Her teeth are pearls.)

CRISPIN.

She's strong –

(He hands her a piece of firewood which she breaks in two.)

ERASTE.

Artistic –

(She takes out a piece of embroidery from the basket.)

CRISPIN.

Kind –

(She tucks **GERONTE***'s shawl around his lap.)*

ERASTE.

She cooks –

(She produces a small cake from the basket.)

CRISPIN.

Recites –

ISABELLE.

How doth the –

CRISPIN.

She's refined!

(She curtsies.)

GERONTE.

Yes, yes, I see her virtues all intact.

But what has this to do with me, in fact?

CRISPIN.

Please tell us, sir, your thoughts on marriage.

GERONTE.

Why?

CRISPIN.

This demoiselle would like to satisfy

Her mother's fondest wish and marry –

GERONTE.

You?

You wish to marry?

ISABELLE.

Yes, I –

GERONTE.

That will do!

CRISPIN.

(Aside to **ERASTE.** *)*

Now! Ask him now!

ERASTE.

I can't. I'm petrified!

You do it.

CRISPIN.

No, it must be you.

ERASTE.

But I'd

Just make him angry. Please!

(*ERASTE gives* **CRISPIN** *a look he uses only when he is so desperate he can think of nothing else. It resembles Kermit when he wrinkles up his mouth. It always works on* **CRISPIN**.)

CRISPIN.

All right!

(*To* **GERONTE**.)

You're satisfied that she should marry?

GERONTE.

Quite.

CRISPIN.

You think a worthy wife she well might be?

GERONTE.

Well, I suppose…

ERASTE.

(*Aside to* **CRISPIN**.)

He likes her!

LISETTE.

Ssh! We'll see.

ERASTE.

I knew he'd do it!

LISETTE.

So did I.

ISABELLE.

And me!

CRISPIN.

Then you approve of her as wife to be?

GERONTE.

I plan to marry her immediately.

ERASTE.

Oh joy!

ISABELLE.

Oh rapture!

LISETTE.

Love!

CRISPIN.

We did it!

ALL FOUR.

(Suddenly realizing at the same time.)

What?

LISETTE.

You?

ERASTE.

Marry her?

CRISPIN.

Yourself?

GERONTE.

Of course. Why not?
That's what you've been suggesting, isn't it?

ERASTE.

But he meant –

CRISPIN.

Well, you see –

LISETTE.

That is –

CRISPIN.

(Aside and very quietly.)

Oh, sh–

GERONTE.

Now that I think on it, a good idea!
In my declining years a wife would be a
Nurse, companion in connubial bliss,

To bathe me, dress me, read to me –

LISETTE.

What's this?

Those are my duties!

GERONTE.

Were. Until today.

You're fired.

LISETTE.

Ha!

GERONTE.

I mean just what I say.

LISETTE.

You constipated, liver-spotted gout–
Infested ancient and decrepit lout!
You can't just toss me out into the street.

GERONTE.

Oh yes I can, you slut. Revenge is sweet.

LISETTE.

And what about the services that I
Perform for you, without which you would die?

GERONTE.

You've just extolled the great intelligence
Of what's-her-name. Her kindness, common sense,
You'll teach her everything before you go.
The poultices and soporifics –

LISETTE.

No!

GERONTE.

You'll do just as I say!

LISETTE.

I won't!

GERONTE.

You will!

You vixen!

LISETTE.

Croaker!

GERONTE.

Brabbler!

LISETTE.

Imbecile!

MME ARGANTE.

Monsieur?!

GERONTE.

Madame?

MME ARGANTE.

I have a word to say.
Before you call my daughter fiancée
I must know that her future is secure.
When marrying a man who is...mature,
As you are, she must have...stability.
You're surely not inclined to disagree.
And, too, my daughter must be given voice.
She has some say in this important choice.

ISABELLE.

I –

MME ARGANTE.

That's enough!

GERONTE.

I bow to your concern.
No doubt you will not be distressed to learn
That though mature, I am still in my prime
Of life, and what is more important, I'm
A very rich old man. My whole estate
I will bequeath to her.

ERASTE.

(Aside.)

Oh, fickle fate!

ISABELLE.

Oh dear!

(She faints. **MME ARGANTE** *and* **ERASTE** *attend her.)*

MME ARGANTE.

She's fainted from the very thrill
Of being wed to you –

CRISPIN.

(Aside.)

And to his will.

MME ARGANTE.

In that case, cher monsieur, it is with pleasure
That I present my daughter's greatest treasure –
Her hand in marriage –

(She and **ERASTE** *carry the still-fainted* **ISABELLE** *over to the old man, offering her limp hand.)*

GERONTE.

(As **ISABELLE** *is reviving.)*

And with rest and care,
We may produce a new and legal heir!

*(***ISABELLE** *faints again.)*

MME ARGANTE.

She's weak from joy.

CRISPIN.

Apparently.

ERASTE.

(Aside to **CRISPIN**.*)*

Crispin!

CRISPIN.

I know. We need to make another plan.

(To **GERONTE.**)

You cannot marry her.

GERONTE.

Why not?

LISETTE.

(Aside to **CRISPIN.**)

　　　　　　　　　Why not?

CRISPIN.

The illness you'll endure –

(Aside to **LISETTE.**)

　　　　　Make up a plot!

LISETTE.

It's quite well known that men in their mature years
Who marry, will undoubtedly endure years
Of symptoms, ills, diseases and conditions
Inflicted by such addle-brained ambitions.

GERONTE.

All well and good, such clever little quips,
But I've not heard it from a doctor's lips.

LISETTE.

(Aside.) A doctor's lips?

(To **GERONTE.**)

　　　　　　　It just so happens I
Have sent for one, to come and testify.

(She is edging **CRISPIN** *toward the study.)*

An expert and a world-renowned physician
Who will himself present his admonition
Regarding marriage after sixty-five.
Just listen if you want to stay alive.

(Aside to **CRISPIN**.*)*

The trunk!

CRISPIN.

The costumes?

LISETTE.

In the study. Go!

You'll be my world-renowned physician!

CRISPIN.

Oh!

I get it! What a perspicacious scheme!

LISETTE.

(He goes. **LISETTE** *takes the focus.)*

This doctor, sir, is held in high esteem
Among his colleagues for his expertise
In matters of infection and disease.

GERONTE.

I want to tend to matters here at hand!
Lisette, explain so that she'll understand
The tasks she will perform as wife and nurse.

LISETTE.

(Aside.)

I'd better humor him.

(To **ISABELLE**.*)*

First, you must curse

Him regularly, just like this –

GERONTE.

Lisette!

LISETTE.

All right! Now every night you have to get
The mustard plaster for his chest. You put
The ointment on right here, next, wrap his foot...

(She lifts the wrapped foot to demonstrate and lets it drop.)

LISETTE.

This one. Like this –

GERONTE.

Ow!

LISETTE.

Please don't interrupt.
He gets six drops of this before he's supped.
And ten of these right afterwards.

ISABELLE.

(She sits, feeling faint.)

Oh, dear!

LISETTE.

(Jerking him forward.)

The cataplasms go on over here.

ISABELLE.

Oh dear!

ERASTE.

*(Aside to **ISABELLE**.)*

Don't fear. Crispin will save the day.

LISETTE.

You give him these just after dejeuner.

ISABELLE.

Oh my!

LISETTE.

(Taking out some enema apparatus.)

And most importantly, you stand
Upon a chair, like this, you raise your hand,
The trick is in the wrist. Like this – parfait!
And then you push –

ERASTE.

(Referring to **ISABELLE.***)*

> She's fainted dead away.

LISETTE.

Imagine that.

MME ARGANTE.

> Wake up!

LISETTE.

> > We'll do the rest

Another day.

MME ARGANTE.

> I think that would be best.

(The doorbell rings.)

LISETTE.

Saved by the bell.

(To them.)

And here's the doctor now!

GERONTE.

Lisette! The door!

LISETTE.

> I'm going, snake-tongue!

GERONTE.

> > > Sow!

(Stopping her before she goes to the door.)

This doctor…is he short?

LISETTE.

> Short?

GERONTE.

> > Short. You know,

A shorter man will charge you less.

LISETTE.

> > Oho!

I should have guessed.

(She goes to the door and opens it so CRISPIN will hear her. We see the doctor's bag peeking in.)

Dear master, I assure you,

That with great care I hastened to procure you...

(Speaking directly out the door to CRISPIN.)

The SHORTEST expert in his discipline.

But see with your own eyes.

(To CRISPIN.)

Please do come in.

(The doctor's bag drops down as CRISPIN sinks to his knees. He enters in a doctor's robe which hangs in hoop fashion to the floor, covering the fact that he is either walking on his knees or squatting.)

CRISPIN.

Zer ahngenamen!

LISETTE.

Same to you. Entrez.

CRISPIN.

(With a thick German accent.)

You zent for me?

LISETTE.

Yah.

CRISPIN.

I came right avay.

LISETTE.

(Introducing him.)

May I present le docteur...

CRISPIN.

(Accent on first syllable) GESundheit.

GERONTE.

Who? GESundheit?

CRISPIN.

Yah, GESundheit. Zat's right.

(Clicking his heels and bowing to everyone.)

Yavol.

MME ARGANTE.

He looks familiar.

CRISPIN.

Ach! Madame!

You look familiar to me too. I am
Remembering a small café in Munich...
You all in blue, and I in my new tunic –
Nein, vait, I vas in lederhosen –
Yah, lederhosen. Ach, my legs were frozen!
But nefermind, ve had a full moon too,
Ve zipped a Schnapps togezer, me and you!

MME ARGANTE.

Oh no, monsieur! It wasn't I!

CRISPIN.

Nein?

MME ARGANTE.

Nein.

CRISPIN.

Vell, zen, perhaps zom eefning you vill dine
Vis me – zat iss, if you're not...

MME ARGANTE.

Married? No.

I'm widowed.

CRISPIN.

Ach! Mein heart iss froelich! *[froy-lick]*

MME ARGANTE.

Oh!

CRISPIN.

(Kisses her hand and clicks his heels.)

But now, ze patient.

LISETTE.

Here.

GERONTE.

(Taking a look at the doctor.)

Wait! What's your fee?

CRISPIN.

Vat doess he zay? He speaks of fees to me?
It vounds mein pride.

*(To **GERONTE**.)*

Mein Herr, please let me zpeak.
I rise up to defend ziss harsh critique.

> *(He tries to rise up, still on his knees, and ends up "standing" on a chair.)*

Accept a fee for practicing mein art?
Ze payment for zuch deeds lies in ze heart.
A doctor serves mit great humility.
Your life und health are in my custody.
To take a fee for zuch a precious gift
Vould rent mine heart und set mine zoul adrift
Upon a sea of shame. My recompense
Is your recovery. Let us commence.

> *(He brings a screen over to conceal them from **MME ARGANTE** and **ISABELLE**.)*

Mein damen, if you'll please to pardon me,
I must conduct zis matter privately.

MME ARGANTE.

Why certainement, monsieur! Au revoir!

ISABELLE.

Au revoir!

CRISPIN.

Auf wiedersoehn!

ERASTE.

Au revoir!

(To **ISABELLE.***)*

I won't be far.

CRISPIN.

Now zen, ze symptoms?

LISETTE.

None as yet, good sir.
But you've been called so that you might aver
The consequences should an older man
Decide to marry late in life.

CRISPIN.

Vorse zan...

Ze plague are all ze pains zat vill ensue
Ven such a deed iss donc. Mein Herr, were you
Considering an action of zis sort?

GERONTE.

Well, I...

CRISPIN.

If zo, I caution you. Abort
All thoughts of such a dreadful undertaking.
A marriage now could vell be your unmaking.

GERONTE.

Ha! Balderdash! As for this vile disease,
Go on with all your rich analyses.
It could not be more vile than constipation,
And marriage has a greater compensation.

CRISPIN.

Perhaps if I described ze symptoms, zen

You might be vell obliged to sink again.

GERONTE.

Go on. Describe away, but you will find
That nothing you may say will change my mind.

CRISPIN.

First off, ze kidney pain –

> (**LISETTE** *jabs him in the back without him seeing her do it.*)

GERONTE.

Ow!

CRISPIN.

Zat's nephritis.

A shrobbing in ze knees –

> *(She gives him a chop in the knees.)*

GERONTE.

Ooh!

CRISPIN.

Zat's phlebitis.

A ringing in ze ears –

> *(She rings a bell near his ears.)*

GERONTE.

How's that?

CRISPIN.

Und now,
Ze vorst: a sticking in ze left side –

> *(She begins poking him with a fire iron.)*

GERONTE.

Ow!

CRISPIN.

A tickling feeling. But you need not fear.
It vill subside, in ten months to a year.

> (**LISETTE** *is poking him as* **ERASTE** *rings the bell.*)

GERONTE.

How dreadful! Doctor?

CRISPIN.

Yah?

GERONTE.

I've not yet wed,

And symptoms manifest themselves!

CRISPIN.

I dread

To sink vat vould occur had you gone through

Vit such a plan, Mein Herr. I caution you –

GERONTE.

But I don't think I –

CRISPIN.

Vat age iss ze bride?

ERASTE.

She's twenty.

CRISPIN.

Ach du lieber! You'd have died!

But not before ze scalp condition.

GERONTE.

Oh!

What happens?

CRISPIN.

Vell, ze hair begins to go.

(**LISETTE** *is cutting from the back of his hair and throwing it in his lap. The bell, kidney pain, and knee chops continue.*)

GERONTE.

Good Heavens! Call the wedding off at once!

LISETTE.

(*Aside to* **CRISPIN.**)

Now this was one of your more brilliant stunts.

But tell me – where'd you get such expertise
In medicine?

               CRISPIN.

          A surgeon, Viennese,
Taught me his whole physician's repertory.
One time we sliced – but that's another story.

       (To **GERONTE.***)*

Observing zat you've now come to your zenses,
I haf enjoyed a doctor's recompenses
And can depart vit lightened heart to see
Another healthy patient cured by me.

          (**LISETTE** *removes the screen as he departs.* **MME ARGANTE** *slips him her name and address.* **ISABELLE** *and* **ERASTE** *slip behind the screen to neck. They do this as often as they are able throughout the scene.)*

          GERONTE.

The strangest doctor!

          LISETTE.

          Yes, indeed.

          MME ARGANTE.

                  But charming.

          GERONTE.

Those symptoms came so suddenly.

          LISETTE.

                  Alarming.

          GERONTE.

They've activated my digestive tract.

          (He gives **LISETTE** *the prearranged signal. She ignores it.)*

          LISETTE.

How interesting.

GERONTE.

I must go, in fact.

LISETTE.

How's that?

GERONTE.

(Doing the signal again.)

It's time!

LISETTE.

Time? Time for what, pray tell?

GERONTE.

(To his guests.)

Excuse me for a moment, I'm not well.

(To **LISETTE.** *)*

Lisette! The water closet!

LISETTE.

Certainly.

Except of course I can't. You fired me.

GERONTE.

What!

LISETTE.

Surely you recall, sir, I've been fired.

Remember? You just told me.

GERONTE.

You're rehired.

Now get me out of here!

(To the guests.)

I shall return

In just a moment –

(To **LISETTE.** *)*

You are going to burn

In hell for this –

LISETTE.

You too!

GERONTE.

I have to go!

LISETTE.

We're going, chowder-head –

GERONTE.

Too slow! Too slow!

A toute à l'heure! Oh hurry!

MME ARGANTE.

A bientôt!

*(**LISETTE** and **GERONTE** exit. **CRISPIN** returns as himself.)*

A most abrupt departure, I must say.

Well, daughter, we must leave without delay.

Now that this marriage plan is nullified

We have no purpose here –

ERASTE.

But madam, I'd…

I'd…well…

MME ARGANTE.

What is it?

ERASTE.

If I might suggest

Myself as suitor –

MME ARGANTE.

I would not protest –

ERASTE.

O, Heaven is my friend!

ISABELLE.

And mine!

CRISPIN.

And mine!

MME ARGANTE.

Except –

ALL THREE.

What?

MME ARGANTE.

You're aware of my design.
I cannot give my daughter's hand away
Without a strong financial resumé.
Tell me, are you the only legal heir?

(**LISETTE** *re-enters.*)

ERASTE.

(*To* **CRISPIN**.)

Am I?

CRISPIN.

Not quite.

LISETTE.

Almost.

MME ARGANTE.

Well then, is there
A legal document of sorts? A will?

ERASTE.

Is there?

CRISPIN.

Not quite.

LISETTE.

Almost.

MME ARGANTE.

Well then, until
You can provide sufficient proof to me
That you're your uncle's only legatee
I cannot sanction such a marriage.

ERASTE & ISABELLE.

Oh!

MME ARGANTE.

Your uncle's fond of you of course –

ERASTE.

Oh no!

I mean –

CRISPIN.

He worships him.

LISETTE.

Adores the boy.

CRISPIN.

His very presence makes him cry –

LISETTE.

– For joy!

CRISPIN.

They're quite insep'rable, those two.

LISETTE.

How true.

GERONTE.

(From offstage.)

Lisette!

LISETTE.

(Exiting.)

Excuse me please.

ERASTE.

(Aside to **CRISPIN.**)

What shall we do?

CRISPIN.

Relax. I'll broach the subject of the will.

(Aside.)

Now this one will require my expert skill.

LISETTE.

(Returning with **GERONTE.***)*

Well, here we are again!

MME ARGANTE.

Monsieur!

GERONTE.

Madame.

MME ARGANTE.

I trust you are quite well again.

GERONTE.

I am.

I offer to you my apologies
For my abrupt departure –

MME ARGANTE.

Monsieur, please.

No need at all.

GERONTE.

And for my change of mind
About the marriage. At my age I find
So many things upset my fragile health
That I would not survive but for –

CRISPIN & LISETTE.

Your wealth.

GERONTE.

How's that?

CRISPIN.

Your wealth. This large estate of yours.
The thing which, after you depart, endures.

GERONTE.

My fortune?

CRISPIN.

Yes.

GERONTE.
Well, what about it?
CRISPIN.

Yes!

GERONTE.
Yes what?!

CRISPIN.
If you'd permit me to express
My thoughts on matters of a legal bent,
You must, monsieur, make clear your last intent
Regarding your estate.
GERONTE.
How's that?
LISETTE.

Your will!
You need to make a will, you imbecile!
GERONTE.
I know that, ninny!

LISETTE.
Fossil!
GERONTE.
Weasel!
LISETTE.

Bat!
CRISPIN.
(With a poke to **LISETTE.***)*
So you've pursued the question, sir, at that.
GERONTE.
I've sent for my solicitors today
To come and write down what I have to say.
ERASTE.
O, day of judgement!
ISABELLE.
Hour of truth!

LISETTE.

Here goes.

CRISPIN.

You wouldn't care to tell us, I suppose,
The nature of this document.

GERONTE.

I plan
To leave my whole estate to a young man…

ERASTE.

O, Heavenly reward!

ISABELLE.

O shining truth!

GERONTE.

A very noble and upstanding youth…
A distant cousin whom I've never seen.

ERASTE.

My soul is dead.

ISABELLE.

O woe!

CRISPIN.

O sorrowed spleen!

LISETTE.

And that is, as they say, the bitter end.

CRISPIN.

Your whole estate to him?

GERONTE.

No. I intend
To leave him half. The other half I leave…
To my cousine Odette.

ERASTE & ISABELLE.

I weep. I grieve!

GERONTE.

I haven't seen her since she was a tot,
But as a tot I liked her quite a lot.

CRISPIN.

Could you have overlooked a close relation?

Who has for you the greatest admiration

And merits from you some consideration?

GERONTE.

You mean my nephew – hapless assignation?

Don't worry, I've a legacy in store

For you. Six hundred francs a year – no more.

MME ARGANTE.

Come, daughter, we must go. We've stayed too long.

ISABELLE.

(To **ERASTE.** *)*

Goodbye.

ERASTE.

Goodbye, my dearest girl.

CRISPIN.

Be strong.

Don't give up hope. This is not over yet.

We'll think of something, me and my Lisette.

GERONTE.

Au revoir, mesdames. A pleasure meeting you.

ISABELLE.

(Curtsying, very sadly.)

Au revoir, monsieur.

(Curtsying to **CRISPIN** *and* **LISETTE.** *)*

Au revoir.

CRISPIN & LISETTE.

Au revoir.

MME ARGANTE.

(Pulling **ISABELLE** *out the door.)*

Adieu!

GERONTE.

Lisette!

LISETTE.

You lizard!

GERONTE.

Dolt! Take me away.

I want my blood let.

LISETTE.

Anything you say.

*(Aside to **ERASTE** who stands frozen.)*

Don't worry. There's a way to get her back.
Crispin and I will plan a new attack.

*(She wheels **GERONTE** off into the study very fast.)*

CRISPIN.

*(Going to **ERASTE**, who is still frozen.)*

Ah, master. Can you speak? Well, this is worse
Than I had thought. Now master, please –

ERASTE.

I curse

The day that I was born!

CRISPIN.

You don't mean that.

ERASTE.

I do.

(Walking to the chair where Isabelle was sitting.)

This is the chair on which she sat.
So close for just a moment we could touch.
And now she's gone forever!

CRISPIN.

(Crying.)

It's too much!

ERASTE.

O flighty fortune, all my life you've been
A sad companion, hovering within

The shadows of my dreams –

CRISPIN.

It's true!

ERASTE.

What sorrows

Come to steal my beautiful tomorrows?

CRISPIN.

How cruel!

ERASTE.

When I first came, so long ago,
I thought that here with uncle I would know
A happiness to soothe my troubled soul.
A home, a family to make me whole.

CRISPIN.

Alas!

ERASTE.

'Twas not to be. I did not grieve,
For deep down Uncle loves me, I believe.
But now, the cruelest stroke of fate has come
To rob me of my dearest wish.

CRISPIN.

I'm numb.

ERASTE.

O solemn solitude! O misery!
I'm going to throw myself into the sea!

CRISPIN.

But master, you're in Paris.

ERASTE.

Oh well then,

I'll go and throw myself into the Seine.

(He exits. **LISETTE** *re-enters.)*

LISETTE.

Will this day never end?!

CRISPIN.

Indeed. How is he?

LISETTE.

How is he? At the moment, weak and dizzy.
What happened to our hero?

CRISPIN.

He's gone out.

To throw himself into the Seine.

LISETTE.

No doubt.

CRISPIN.

We've got to help him. Somehow.

LISETTE.

Yes, we should.

When all is said and done that lad is –

BOTH.

Good.

LISETTE.

Well?

CRISPIN.

Well?

LISETTE.

Let's see…

CRISPIN.

What are we going to do?

LISETTE.

We need a plan.

CRISPIN.

I'm looking right at you.

LISETTE.

(They start pacing.)

Hmm.

CRISPIN.

Hmm.

LISETTE.

The legal heir.

CRISPIN.

Geronte…

LISETTE.

Mamá…

CRISPIN.

Eraste and Isabelle –

LISETTE.

The will – Aha!

Two distant cousins…

(She begins walking him toward the study.)

CRISPIN.

One he's never seen…

LISETTE.

The other as a child –

CRISPIN.

What can you mean?

LISETTE.

Two yokels from the country –

CRISPIN.

No doubt crass –

LISETTE.

One of them has a voice to shatter glass –
The trunk.

(She sends him into the study. He brings back the trunk.)

CRISPIN.

The trunk?

(She opens the trunk.)

LISETTE.

The costumes.

CRISPIN.

(Finally gets it.)

Et voila!

LISETTE.

A dowager from Brest –

CRISPIN.

And a bourgeois.
Now how does one persuade a dying man
With faulty reason to amend his plan
And leave his whole estate to someone who
Deserves it?

LISETTE.

We arrange a rendez-vous
With cousins –

(She is pulling costumes from the trunk.)

CRISPIN.

Who themselves will fast persuade
Geronte to have them put in the stockade!

LISETTE.

Now let me see. Well, well! What have we here!
A lovely costume –

CRISPIN.

If you're doing Lear.

LISETTE.

Oh. What about this one? What am I bid?
Ten sous? Fifteen?

CRISPIN.

No, no, it's too...El Cid.

LISETTE.

And this?

CRISPIN.

Too somber. It just isn't me.
Unless, of course, I'm doing Richard Three.

LISETTE.

You played the tragedies?

CRISPIN.

I used to act.

I toured with Jean-Baptiste Poquelin, in fact.

LISETTE.

(With utmost reverence, crossing themselves again.)

Molière?!

CRISPIN.

The master.

LISETTE.

Live on stage?

CRISPIN.

What glory!

That third act when – but that's another story.

LISETTE.

(Holding up a garish woman's costume.)

Well, now, the only thing that seems to fit
Is this. It suits you well, I must admit.

CRISPIN.

Now wait a minute!

LISETTE.

You're a Thespian.

What diff'rence if you play a maid or man?
In England all the boys play Juliet!

CRISPIN.

I can't!

LISETTE.

You must. You will, Cousine Odette.

CRISPIN.

Well, what about the other one?

LISETTE.

Aha!

We need a costume totally bourgeois.

(Holding up an outrageous country bumpkin costume.)

CRISPIN.

The perfect thing!

LISETTE.

It's hideous.

CRISPIN.

It's small.

LISETTE.

Small?

CRISPIN.

Listen! Can't you hear the Muses call?

LISETTE.

Oh no I can't!

CRISPIN.

Your style, your great panache…

A subtle change of hair, a large moustache –

LISETTE.

You're mad! I've never acted!

CRISPIN.

It's a lark.

I've always thought you had that special spark.

LISETTE.

You did?

CRISPIN.

A face like that, those eyes aflame?

The critics would have thundered with acclaim.

LISETTE.

You think?

CRISPIN.

I know. Besides, who else is there?

He cannot wait to meet...cousin Robert! *[koo-**zan** Row-**bair**]*

> *(He slaps a man's hat on her head as the lights:)*
>
> *(Blackout.)*

Scene Two

(There is a brief blackout with some interlude music.* When the lights come up again, **GERONTE** *speaks from offstage.)*

GERONTE.

(Offstage.) Lisette! Where is that girl? Come here! Crispin!

(He enters, propelling his own wheelchair with arm levers, causing him to go around in circles because of the paralysis in his right arm.)

Oh, why do they torment a dying man?

(He speaks to the audience.)

It's dreadful to be old – it makes me sick!
I've turned into a raving lunatic
Who lives by drips and drops and medications,
Ridiculous concoctions and libations
They give to me to keep the mask of death
From creeping up and stealing my last breath.
In every organ pain and illness lurks.
I haven't got a moving part that works!
My liver would not function but for these,
This for my heart, and these for when I wheeze.
The drops are for my kidneys and my spleen,
The doctor swears the worst he's ever seen!
I cannot move my arm, I need a glass
To see and all day long I'm filled with gas!
Old age is hon'rable, or so they say,
In honor then I watch myself decay
And fade like autumn's rose. At every chance
I close my eyes and slip into a trance.

(He dozes, starts to snore, and wakes himself up.)

---

*Licensees should create an original composition or use music in the public domain.

GERONTE.

I wasn't always as you see me now,
With time and trial written on my brow,
Old age, the crown of life – well, it's a lie!
What future for an old man but to die?
In fact there are the skepticals who bet
That I **am** dead and no one's told me yet!
So I go on and on, day after day,
Dependent on Lisette to ease my way –

(The doorbell rings.)

Somebody get the door! Lisette, you dunce!
Crispin! Come open up the door at once!
An old man at the mercy of such rabble,
No wonder, is it, that I drool and babble!
A bunch of trifling ingrates – who is there?!
Come in then! Oh those worthless proletaire!

LISETTE.

(Entering, disguised as Cousin Robert.)

Hello? Hello?

GERONTE.

Hello?

LISETTE.

How do you do?!

GERONTE.

Who's there?

LISETTE.

Who's where?

GERONTE.

There?

LISETTE.

Here?

GERONTE.

Here!

LISETTE.

Who are you?

GERONTE.

Geronte.

LISETTE.

Geronte?

GERONTE.

Geronte!

LISETTE.

Geronte?

GERONTE.

Geronte!

(They point to each other through this exchange and get mixed up. This entire scene should be played as a Marx-Brothers-meets-Lucy routine. **LISETTE** *is wearing an outlandish country bumpkin costume, including a mirror attached to a string, which she looks into to see who she is. Also a handkerchief, wine bottle, even perhaps a horn. She holds up the mirror to* **GERONTE**'s *face.)*

LISETTE.

That's you, Geronte?

GERONTE.

That's me! What do you want?

LISETTE.

What do **you** want?

GERONTE.

I...don't remember!

LISETTE.

Oh.

Then why did you just call me?

GERONTE.

I don't know!

I'm so confused!

LISETTE.

I know, we'll start again!

(Very slowly.)

Who...are...you?

GERONTE.

I'm...Monsieur... Geronte.

LISETTE.

Well then,

It's you I came to see!

GERONTE.

But who are you?

LISETTE.

I'm...

(Looks in mirror again.)

Your cousin Robert! *[French pronunciation.]*

GERONTE.

No! Is this true?!

(She pumps his hand vigorously and kisses him roughly on both cheeks.)

LISETTE.

Is what true?

GERONTE.

You're cousin Robert?

LISETTE.

Who, me?

GERONTE.

But you just said –

LISETTE.

I did? Then I must be!

Can it be possible? At last I'm here!

*(She blows her nose loudly into the handkerchief, then gives it to **GERONTE**, who drops it in disgust.)*

GERONTE.

Why have you come?

LISETTE.

You'll find out.

GERONTE.

Please, my ear.

What's that you said?

LISETTE.

(Shouting in his ear.)

To VISIT!

GERONTE.

Ow! Watch out!

LISETTE.

(Jumping into his lap in mock fear.)

Watch out for what?

GERONTE.

My foot! I've got the gout!

LISETTE.

(Picking up his foot, then dropping it.)

He does!

GERONTE.

The man's a maniac!

LISETTE.

You think?

GERONTE.

You're acting like a fool!

LISETTE.

Let's have a drink!

*(**LISETTE** lifts the attached wine bottle, uncorks it with her teeth, guzzles a little, then opens **GERONTE**'s mouth and pours some in. He swallows and sputters appropriately. She claps him on the back.)*

GERONTE.

Aaarrgh! He's killing me!

LISETTE.

Let's have some more!

GERONTE.

No please! No more! What have you come here for?

LISETTE.

What for? What for?

(She paces, bangs her fists on tables to try and remember.)

Ah! I'm your legatee!

You're leaving half of your estate to me!

GERONTE.

How did you know?

LISETTE.

News travels fast.

GERONTE.

Indeed.

LISETTE.

The deed?

GERONTE.

The deed?

LISETTE.

The deed is what I need!

GERONTE.

What for?

LISETTE.

To see how much I'm going to get.

Ten thousand francs will pull me out of debt.

GERONTE.

You owe ten thousand francs?

LISETTE.

Shh. Yes, I do.

My creditors are coming after you!

GERONTE.

My God! They're coming here?

LISETTE.

(Jumping into his lap again.)

Who?!

GERONTE.

I don't know!

I'm going mad!

LISETTE.

You are?

GERONTE.

Yes!

LISETTE.

Well, let's go!

(She pushes him around and around in the chair.)

GERONTE.

Go where?

LISETTE.

Go mad!

GERONTE.

The man's a lunatic!

LISETTE.

(Looking in the mirror again.)

I am? I am!

GERONTE.

I'm getting very sick.

LISETTE.

He's getting sick! Well, isn't that divine!
If you die now, then all this will be mine!

(She begins to stuff her large pockets with things.)

GERONTE.

Yes, yes, I promise! All I own will be

Bequeathed to you!

LISETTE.

Then I'm the legatee!

I think I'll cry again!

(She slobbers all over him.)

GERONTE.

Stop that, at once!

LISETTE.

(Stopping abruptly.)

All right.

GERONTE.

You know what you are?

LISETTE.

What?

GERONTE & LISETTE.

A dunce!

LISETTE.

A dunce I am! Oh I'm a dunce, it's true!
And now it's time to say farewell to you!

(She throws the blanket over his head.)

I'll smother you like this until you die…
And then I'll be your legatee…goodbye!

(She slams the door, staying in the room, and begins to remove the costume.)

GERONTE.

Goodbye! Good riddance!

LISETTE.

(As Robert.)

Are you dead yet?

GERONTE.

No!

LISETTE.

What's taking you so long?! Come on, let's go!

GERONTE.

I want to die in peace. Alone.

LISETTE.

All right.

I'll send some men to bury you tonight.

GERONTE.

All right! Tonight! Now go!

LISETTE.

Don't carry on!

I'm going…going…going…going…

(She slams the door again.)

GERONTE.

Gone!

Good God, the man's a raving maniac!
I nearly had a fatal heart attack!
And where is everyone when most I need them?
Lisette! Crispin! I shelter them, I feed them,
And this is what I get for gratitude.
I've got to have that lunatic pursued!
He's dangerous! Lisette!

LISETTE.

(Re-entering as herself.)

What now, old crust?

GERONTE.

Where were you?

LISETTE.

At the market. And I just
Walked in the door and you're berating me!

GERONTE.

Oh never mind. Lisette, such devilry

Was standing in this room just now.

LISETTE.

Just when?

GERONTE.

Before you came.

LISETTE.

Before! Who was it, then?

GERONTE.

My relative, cousin Robert.

LISETTE.

Robert!

Imagine that! Right here? Right where?

GERONTE.

Right there!

He pranced around, he slobbered on my clothes,
Drank wine, made noise, he babbled, blew his nose,
An idiot! With wild and frenzied ways.

LISETTE.

And he's to be one of your protegés?

GERONTE.

Not any longer. I have changed my mind.
A foolish choice. How could I be so blind?
Well, I shall not succumb to idle threat.
I'll leave my whole estate to dear Odette.
That fellow was ambitious, but his itch
Is no match for this man who's old and rich.

(The doorbell rings.)

Now what?! That doorbell hasn't stopped all day!
Go tell whoever's there to go away.

LISETTE.

Indeed I will. Let's see, what shall I say?

(Opening the door.)

Monsieur Geronte won't see you. Go away!

(**CRISPIN** *pushes himself in. He is an eighteenth-century Tootsie.*)

CRISPIN.

Yoo hoo! Is anyone at home?

GERONTE.

Now who?

CRISPIN.

Mon Dieu! Cousin Geronte! Can it be you?

GERONTE.

I –

CRISPIN.

Yes, it is! My heart's abrim with tears,
To see my cousin after all these years

GERONTE.

Extraordinary! Here's the other one!
She seems more pleasant –

CRISPIN.

(Aside.)

Wait, I've just begun.

(To him.)

Yes, I, cousine Odette, came all this way
To pay my deep respects to you today.

GERONTE.

Polite as well. Lisette! Get her a chair.

CRISPIN.

A chair?! In your great presence? I'll sit there.

(He takes a small ottoman and settles himself in.)

That's better.

GERONTE.

Quite an ample woman, she.

LISETTE.

I think she looks divine, if you ask me.

CRISPIN.

I beg your pardon?

GERONTE.

I was just observing

How fine your figure is, so large, so...

LISETTE.

(Grabbing one of his fake breasts.)

Curving.

CRISPIN.

You think so?

GERONTE.

Very charming.

CRISPIN.

(Smacking him hard with her fan.)

Fie, you jest!

GERONTE.

Ow! Strong, she is!

LISETTE.

And filled with ample...

(With her face very close to his fake breasts.)

ZEST...

CRISPIN.

I look too dreadful! Marriage is a chore.

It's my accurs'd condition I deplore.

A widow and a mother and at twenty.

GERONTE.

How many children have you?

CRISPIN.

I have...plenty.

Sixteen to be exact.

GERONTE.

Mon Dieu! Astounding!

LISETTE.

Indeed.

GERONTE.

Odette, you have good health abounding.

To have so many children, and before

The age of twenty-one.

CRISPIN.

I had but four.

The rest I've had since my poor husband died.

GERONTE.

Then you remarried.

CRISPIN.

No! I can't abide

The thought of wounding my late husband's ghost.

GERONTE.

But then your children are –

CRISPIN.

Monsieur! A host

Does not presume to criticize his guest.

GERONTE.

How do you manage?

CRISPIN.

There, I have been blessed

With quite a satifact'ry revenue.

GERONTE.

What do you do?

LISETTE.

What do you do?

CRISPIN.

I sue!

GERONTE.

You sue?

LISETTE.

She sues?

CRISPIN.

I sue.

GERONTE.

I see. But who?

CRISPIN.

Who?

GERONTE.

Who?

LISETTE.

Who do you sue?

CRISPIN.

Why, everyone!

GERONTE.

A most bizarre métier.

LISETTE.

I'll say.

CRISPIN.

And none
Escape my legal wrath once I decide
To sue, pursue, persist and have them tried.
In fact, Monsieur, I ought to make it clear
That it's precisely what has brought me here.

GERONTE.

You're suing someone?

CRISPIN.

Yes, I am.

GERONTE.

But who?

CRISPIN.

Who do I sue?

LISETTE.

Who do you sue?

CRISPIN.

Why, you!

GERONTE.

Me?!

LISETTE.

Him?

CRISPIN.

None other.

GERONTE.

You? Sue me? For what?

CRISPIN.

I am your legal cousin, am I not?

GERONTE.

Unfortunately.

CRISPIN.

But indeed it's so.

I must protect my interests, you know.

You're old, you're miserly, and in the main,

It's obvious you're incurably insane.

LISETTE.

How true.

GERONTE.

What do I hear?

CRISPIN.

I cannot chance

You wasting all of my inheritance,

So I shall sue for every sou you own

And this estate will come to me alone.

GERONTE.

I'm going mad!

CRISPIN.

You see? I'm clearly right.

I've sent for men to cart you off tonight.

GERONTE.

You what?!

CRISPIN.

Now, now, what use for such a protest?
In certum est quod certum reddi potest.

LISETTE.

How true.

GERONTE.

In what?

CRISPIN.

Cousin *[koo-ZAN]* do not dispute a
Matter quite pecunia constituta.

GERONTE.

Do I have that disease?

LISETTE.

I think you do.

CRISPIN.

(Starting to throw legal papers at him.)

A pactum commisorium for you.

GERONTE.

Lisette! Do something! Oh, I'm getting sick!

CRISPIN.

Or else a bannitio *[banni TEE-oh]*. Take your pick.

GERONTE.

How did such vile relations come to be
In this upstanding bourgeois family?

ERASTE.

(Bursting in the door, soaking wet.)

O cursèd life!

(Seeing **CRISPIN** *and not recognizing him.)*

I beg your pardon.

CRISPIN.

Oh!

Who's this?

GERONTE.

My nephew.

CRISPIN.

Is this embryo

Included in the will?

GERONTE.

A modest sum.

Six hundred francs a year.

CRISPIN.

What's this? Come come!

He doesn't get a sou! I won't allow it.

LISETTE.

Another loving relative. And now it

Seems as though she's running your estate.

Such relatives one must appreciate.

LISETTE, CRISPIN & GERONTE.

(*Noticing* **ERASTE**'s *condition.*)

You're wet.

ERASTE.

I know. I...fell into the Seine.

If you'll excuse me, ladies, gentlemen...

(*He stops as he's leaving and stares at* **CRISPIN**.)

Crispin!

GERONTE.

What's that?

ERASTE.

That is – I mean –

LISETTE.

Creased pants.

His pants are creased. In fact he's all askance.

This is your uncle's **cousin** [English pron.] come to claim
The whole of Uncle's fortune in her name.

CRISPIN.

Monsieur, there's naught that happens accidare. [ak-si-DAH-ray]
Ergo, you must consent to acceptare [ak-sep–TAR-ay]
Or else I'll have you rendered ab agendo.

GERONTE.

Ab-what?

CRISPIN.

Incapable. In ex provendo.
Therefore I must serve you a force et armus.

GERONTE.

Lisette! I think she really means to harm us!

CRISPIN.

Au revoir, cousin *[Koo-zan]*, in two days I'll take action,
And have you taken from here by abaction.

(*Explaining.*)

Brute force.

GERONTE.

Good God!

LISETTE.

My word!

CRISPIN.

Abalienate. *[abal-yen AH-tay]*
I'll see you, sir, in short, in court.

(*He takes a bite of the hors d'oeuvres as he leaves.*)

Good paté. *[PAH-tay]*

(*He exits.*)

GERONTE.

Could anyone have been so cruelly blest
With such relations?

LISETTE.

I was unimpressed.

GERONTE.

Abalienate! Is it catching?

LISETTE.

No.

GERONTE.

I can't believe they want to overthrow
My whole estate before I'm dead and gone!
I've never seen such dreadful goings-on.
They've aggravated my digestive tract,
My spleen, my kidneys and my heart, in fact!

LISETTE.

A shame. They bring an old man to his death.

GERONTE.

As long as those two vultures draw a breath
Upon this earth, I'll live in mortal fear.

LISETTE.

As well you should.

CRISPIN.

(Returning as himself.)

What's going on in here?

GERONTE.

Lisette! I'm dying! Take me to my room!

LISETTE.

He's off again.

CRISPIN.

(Aside to **ERASTE.** *)*

All hail the bride and groom.

GERONTE.

Such terrible relations!

LISETTE.

Yes, indeed.

GERONTE.

I'll have them flogged!

LISETTE.

Such viciousness, such greed!

(To **ERASTE** *and* **CRISPIN.***)*

I'll take him up from here.

GERONTE.

Crackbrain!

LISETTE.

Dumbbell!

ERASTE.

Oh uncle, I'm so sorry you're not well!

GERONTE.

Another relative! I curse them all!

LISETTE.

Stay downstairs. If I need you I will call.

(She exits with **GERONTE.***)*

ERASTE.

I'm so upset.

CRISPIN.

But why? There's no one left
To leave his fortune to. He is bereft
Of relatives except for you, my master.

ERASTE.

You mean, again you've saved me from disaster?

CRISPIN.

I have. But please, no thanks. To have your dream
Be realized, I'd stoop to any scheme.

ERASTE.

You've saved my heart from ruin and despair.
My gratitude –

CRISPIN.

The answer to my prayer –

ERASTE.

Is boundless.

CRISPIN.

Oh, I need no gratitude.

(Aside.)

I'm in a very, very happy mood.

ERASTE.

There must be some way I can thank you.

CRISPIN.

Well,

Some gesture might turn up, sir. Time will tell.

*(***LISETTE*** *bursts into the room.* **CRISPIN** *and* **ERASTE** *turn and look at her.)*

What's wrong?

LISETTE.

We overdid it.

ERASTE.

What?

LISETTE.

The trick.

We made him just a little bit too sick.

CRISPIN.

How sick?

LISETTE.

Quite sick.

ERASTE.

Where is he?

LISETTE.

In his bed.

CRISPIN.

Exactly what is wrong with him?

LISETTE.

He's dead.

(Blackout.)

End of Act I

ACT II

Scene One

(About an hour later. **CRISPIN** *is sitting, quietly, reading Shakespeare.* **ERASTE** *paces.)*

ERASTE.

Oh, dirty death! You come to rob me of
My only uncle's favor – nay, his love!
Yet I would love him not or be not loved
By one most dear to me. My heart is gloved
In ebon cloths, as wretchedly it beats
For Isabelle. Then, sadly, it retreats
From those sweet lips of ruby, hair of honey
Which love forsake for lack of uncle's money.
Yet were he to bestow upon me such
At his demise, I would not love to touch
For loss of uncle's love. Oh, by my oath,
Why am I not allowed to love them both?
And yet, I do, the agéd and the fair,
And loving two, yet am I solitaire.
Injustice most injurious, unkind!
The tears you fill my eyes with do not blind
My aching soul to fortune and despair.
To win her hand, for him I must not care,
But wish him dead and in that wish disown
My uncle's love. Oh Gods! I am alone.

CRISPIN.

(Putting down his book.)

An interesting paradox, 'twould seem.

Untimely death – a classic, tragic theme
In this rich tapestry of life we weave,
For what is death? What life? What use to grieve?
The problem, nay dilemma for digestion:
To be or not to be, that is the question.
You know, 'tis common, all who live must die.
There is no mercy in it, ask not why,
But rather think on this, so oft refrained:
The quality of mercy is not strained.
It is the well-expected – all must learn:
O yesterday! Do not bid time return!
And so it goes with old Geronte.
Death laughs, and talks of graves and worms and epitaphs.
The whips and scorns of time do give him strife,
The great calamity of so long life.
This issue has an int'resting morale,
Recalling words of my old friend Pascal,
Who, in a dialogue, once said to me,
"I think, therefore I am." Quel prosody!
"My friend," he said, "Life's but an allegory.
Ephemeral –" but that's another story.

(**LISETTE** *enters.*)

What news, Lisette?

LISETTE.

What news, he wants to know.

He picked a very awkward time to go.

ERASTE.

Oh destiny! Demonic evildoer!

CRISPIN.

O death, great leveler. What could be truer?

LISETTE.

Philosophy and poetry are nice,
But what we need is practical advice.

We've got a dead man on our hands! What's more,
The notaries are nearly at the door
To take a deposition. Better still,
Without Geronte we haven't got a will.
Without a will, the lovebirds, he and she
Because of mama cannot married be.
If they don't marry, we don't marry – merde!
Well, I feel better now that I have aired
My sentiments. But what are we to do?

     (To CRISPIN.*)*

Don't sit there smirking! We depend on you!

ERASTE.

We ought to call the doctors.

CRISPIN.

             No, not yet.

LISETTE.

We must do something!

CRISPIN.

            Oui, mon alouette.

But what? I've pondered, paced and I've reviewed,
And what I have been able to conclude
Is that the game is up. Fini. Kaput.

ERASTE.

Not even just a tiny scheme afoot?

CRISPIN.

To filch a will in which you were ill-treated,
Now there I can maneuver undefeated.
A sleight of hand and pfft! It's gone.

ERASTE.

             I know.

CRISPIN.

A master clown and impressario.
But doing the reverse! To cause to be

A thing that isn't yet, that's demonry.

ERASTE.

I'm riddled with despair.

LISETTE.

(Going to the window.)

Just wait, there's more.

ERASTE.

What more?

LISETTE.

The notaries are at the door.

(The doorbell rings.)

ERASTE.

Crispin! Do something!

LISETTE.

Should I let them in?

CRISPIN.

Yes. No! Yes! Wait a moment. I begin...
To see... Do they know Uncle's dead?

LISETTE.

Not yet.

CRISPIN.

Perhaps in somber light, a silhouette...

LISETTE.

Well? Should I bring them in?

ERASTE.

Ssh, he's creating.

CRISPIN.

All right, my little cabbage, Keep them waiting.
Let's see now, which attack would be the best?
An honest intrigue, openly expressed?
No, no. An artifice. A subtle bawd.
Enough to – yes, but not a total fraud.
An insignificant deceit – a cunning.

Of course I could – but oh, that would be stunning!
What is it that we need? We need Geronte!
And I say we should give them what they want.
Or else a strong facsimile thereof.

(Going to the costume trunk.)

That's it! A master plan!

(To **LISETTE**.*)*

Come here, my dove.
Go get one of his nightshirts, and a hat.

(To **ERASTE**.*)*

You! Close the drapes.

(Putting his hand to his head.)

My hair! I'll tend to that.

(He gets a wig from the trunk.)

Blow out the candles! Get his blanket too.
We'll have an air-tight will before I'm through.
Now, move the chair into the shadows. Good.

(He transforms himself into **GERONTE**.*)*

CRISPIN.

Well, children, help me sit down if you would.
Today an old man gives his testament.
My last and final will.

LISETTE.

Magnificent!

CRISPIN.

You see a new Geronte born here. To us
He's sympathetic, kind and generous.
And ready for the melancholy visit
Of unkind death.

LISETTE.

Your timing is exquisite.

CRISPIN.

(To **LISETTE** *as she goes to the door.)*

Which arm is paralyzed?

LISETTE.

The right.

CRISPIN.

The right.

(To **ERASTE** *as the lawyers come in.)*

My nephew, I may go yet still tonight,
But my old conscience will not rest until
I have secured your future with a will.
And here are my old faithful notaries.
Good gentlemen, I may begin to wheeze,
But try to write down everything I say,
I must attend this business right away,
For any moment could be my last one.
Sit down please.

(The **NOTARIES**, *very short, with hooped capes to hide the fact that they're on their knees, sit on stools.)*

LISETTE.

(Aside.)

This is going to be fun.

CRISPIN.

I'm glad to see you both in robust health.
I would not be disposing of my wealth
Were I in such a form as yours.

NOTARY.

Merci.

(To his brother.)

He says we're very healthy, brother.

PIERRE.

Oui.

NOTARY.

But as to your condition, sir, don't fear.
The testament which you are giving here
Will give you such an inner quietude
Your heart will heal itself – be reimbued
With youthful verve. Is that not so, Pierre?

PIERRE.

Is what so?

NOTARY.

What I just said!

PIERRE.

Oui, mon frere.

NOTARY.

But let us, gentlemen, complete our chore.
Young lady, please go out and shut the door.

LISETTE.

Not on your life! I cannot leave this man.
He's dying!

CRISPIN.

Gentlemen, fear not, you can
Speak freely in the presence of my maid.
I trust her with my life.

LISETTE.

(Aside to **CRISPIN.***)*

Quel escapade.

PIERRE.

Irregular.

NOTARY.

I know, Pierre, but we
Are paid by him a…modest…salary

To carry out his every wish, n'est-ce pas?
Proceed, monsieur. You write, Pierre.

PIERRE.

Who, moi?

NOTARY.

Yes, vous!

(He hands him a pen and ink and paper.)

CRISPIN.

First off, my debts are to be paid.

PIERRE.

(Writing.)
Debts paid...

CRISPIN.

A certain merchant renegade
Insists I owe him forty francs for wine,
But I am sure it's thirty-five.

LISETTE.

The swine!

PIERRE.

(Writing.)

The swine...

NOTARY.

Monsieur, what sort of funeral
Have you in mind?

CRISPIN.

I've lived a life that's full.
A simple ceremony will suffice,
Which leaves more money for my heirs.

LISETTE.

How nice.

NOTARY.

And now, monsieur, do tell us, if you please,

What are the gifts, bequests and legacies
You wish to have inscribed into your will?

CRISPIN.

To someone who with goodness did fulfill
The role of nephew, loving tenderly,
I name residuary legatee...
My nephew.

ERASTE.

(Forgetting that this is not his uncle.)

Uncle! I don't want your wealth!
I wish I could restore you to good health!

PIERRE.

(Writing and crying.)

Good health...

CRISPIN.

There, there, my boy, no tears for me!
I leave him everything! My property,
The furniture, the contracts and the goods,
The house in Deauville, with surrounding woods...

PIERRE.

Surrounding woods...

CRISPIN.

I disinherit all
My other heirs, thereto and therewithal
From any claim to my estate.

PIERRE.

Estate...

NOTARY.

Well, that sums up the will quite nicely.

CRISPIN.

Wait!
I wish to leave a gift to my Lisette.

LISETTE.

(Weeping copiously.)

Oh master!

CRISPIN.

Did you think I would forget
The hours of toil in which you served me well?
Two thousand crowns in cash to mademoiselle.

ERASTE.

Two thousand!

CRISPIN.

So that she may married be
To her Crispin.

LISETTE.

Your generosity

Is stunning.

ERASTE.

Well, **I'm** stunned.

LISETTE.

May Heaven bless

Your soul.

(To **ERASTE.***)*

Your uncle is a saint.

ERASTE.

Oh, yes.

CRISPIN.

The truth is, I was always miserly.
And miserly's a sinful thing to be.
So I must now atone for such a sin.

LISETTE.

I knew there was a good man deep within
That crusty old exterior.

NOTARY.

And now,

If that is all –

CRISPIN.

Not quite. If you'll allow,
I have one more bequest to make.

PIERRE.

One more…

ERASTE.

One more?

LISETTE.

One more.

CRISPIN.

I should have said before.
To someone who has been a faithful servant,
Attentive, kind, intelligent, observant,
Who's served my nephew faithfully for years,
A man unparalleled by his peers,
Un homme honnete, in short, an honest man,
I'm speaking of that bon vivant –

ERASTE.

Crispin?
How much do you intend to leave him?

CRISPIN.

Oh,
Not much. But some small sum is apropos.
When I remember what he's done for you,
Is doing at this very moment, true?
Your heart's desire is what he longs to see.
Therefore I think a small annuity…

PIERRE & LISETTE.

Annuity…

CRISPIN.

Of fifteen hundred francs
A year would best express my humble thanks.

What do you say, my boy?

ERASTE.

I acquiesce.

CRISPIN.

You're positive you're satisfied?

ERASTE.

Oh yes.

CRISPIN.

Then that concludes the writing of this will.
And now I must be off. I'm feeling ill.

NOTARY.

But sir, the will is void unless you sign.

CRISPIN.

Monsieur, an illness which attacked my spine
Has paralyzed my arm.

PIERRE.

His arm...

NOTARY.

A shame.

An "X" right here will be sufficient name.

CRISPIN.

My fingers move a bit.

LISETTE.

I'll hold your hand.

CRISPIN.

*(Grabbing her breast with his good one, unseen by
the notaries.)*

My darling girl.

LISETTE.

Your wish is my command.

NOTARY.

And there we are.

(He picks up the will.)

PIERRE.

And there we are.

NOTARY.

Fini.

Don't worry sir, leave everything to me.

CRISPIN.

(Grabbing the will.)

I'll keep it here.

NOTARY.

Oh no, sir, you cannot.

We've got to make a copy on the spot.

We shall return posthaste and bring you here

The duplicate.

CRISPIN.

Oh.

NOTARY.

Now, be of good cheer.

Au revoir, monsieur.

PIERRE.

Au revoir, monsieur!

CRISPIN, LISETTE & ERASTE.

Au revoir!

(The **NOTARIES** *exit.)*

LISETTE.

You did it!

ERASTE.

Formidab'! *[for-me-DAB]*

CRISPIN.

Spectacular.

ERASTE.

I must tell Isabelle!

(He starts to leave.)

LISETTE.

My bull.

CRISPIN.

My lamb.

LISETTE.

My duck!

CRISPIN.

My swan!

LISETTE.

My stag!

CRISPIN.

My ewe!

LISETTE.

My ram!

(They embrace passionately.)

ERASTE.

(Stopping as he is about to exit.)

Two thousand crowns? Plus an annuity?

CRISPIN.

He doesn't like the small discrepancy.

LISETTE.

Nor I. The whole thing makes me very tense.
In fact, if we had any common sense
We'd call them back and tell the truth.

ERASTE.

Oh, no!

CRISPIN.

You think, then, we should leave things status quo?

ERASTE.

Oh yes, I'm sure you've handled it correctly.

CRISPIN.

I think so too, sir.

ERASTE.

I'll be back directly.

(He exits.)

LISETTE.

You brilliant man!

CRISPIN.

Yes, I was rather good.

Bonjour, ma femme!

LISETTE.

Adieu to spinsterhood!

I hear the church bells singing out our marriage!

CRISPIN.

A house with servants – and a horse and carriage!

LISETTE.

Our weekends in the country –

CRISPIN.

Ride to hounds –

LISETTE.

A coach and four –

CRISPIN.

And lots of money!

LISETTE.

Mounds.

CRISPIN.

A brand new gown for you –

LISETTE.

With matching hat –

CRISPIN.

An alabaster vase by Monserrat –

A joyous celebration at our wedding –

LISETTE.

The finest woven linens for our bedding –

(They kiss.)

LISETTE.

A ruby ring –

CRISPIN.

A leather moneybag –

LISETTE.

A sumptuous life –

ERASTE.

(Bursting in with **ISABELLE.***)*

We've hit another snag!

CRISPIN.

So much for dreams.

LISETTE.

What happened now?

ISABELLE.

It's Mother.

ERASTE.

Mother's going to pledge her to another
Unless I can provide security
That I'm...

CRISPIN AND LISETTE.

Residuary legatee.

CRISPIN.

(To **LISETTE.***)*

What have we got?

LISETTE.

Well, there's his cashbox.

CRISPIN.

Where?

LISETTE.

(Pointing to the study.)
In there.

CRISPIN.

In there?

(He goes to the room.)

LISETTE.

In there.

(CRISPIN sneaks into the room, emerges with the cashbox, brings it downstage, sets it on the table, and they all gather around it.)

ERASTE.

But do we dare?

LISETTE.

Compared to what we've done so far today,
The taking of his cashbox is soufflé.

ERASTE.

Well then...

ISABELLE.

Well then...

ERASTE.

(Trying to open it.)

It's locked.

CRISPIN & LISETTE.

It's locked.

ISABELLE.

Uh – oh.

CRISPIN.

Where is the key?

ISABELLE.

The key!

LISETTE.

I think I know.
Around his neck he wears a little chain.

CRISPIN, ERASTE & ISABELLE.

And?

LISETTE.

And,

It holds a little key.

CRISPIN.

Give me your hand.

*(**LISETTE** does. He kisses it.)*

Go get it.

(She goes upstairs to Geronte's room.)

Well, I think we've won the game.

ERASTE.

The gods with admiration will proclaim
Your stunning victory, Crispin.

CRISPIN.

Oh, well,

'Twas just a day's work, master, mademoiselle.
Just like the time the colonel said to me,
"Go out and lead the field artillery!"
The battle raged for days – oh, it was gory,
Then at the end – but that's another story.

LISETTE.

*(Bursting out of Geronte's room, standing there,
frozen.)*

Guess what?

CRISPIN.

Now what?

ERASTE.

What now?

LISETTE.

He isn't dead.

CRISPIN, ERASTE & ISABELLE.

Not dead?!

LISETTE.

That's right. What's more, he's not in bed.

He's gone.

CRISPIN.

Gone?

ERASTE & ISABELLE.

Where?

LISETTE.

I don't know, but not far.

He's in this house somewhere.

CRISPIN.

This is bizarre.

(They all begin looking for him, furtively. **LISETTE**
goes back upstairs.)

LISETTE.

We've got to find him quick.

CRISPIN.

Not here.

ISABELLE.

Not here.

CRISPIN.

Monsieur Geronte?

LISETTE.

I'd like to tweak his ear.

ISABELLE.

Yoo hoo!

ERASTE.

Oh Uncle?

LISETTE.

How did he revive?

When I left him that man was not alive!

CRISPIN.

He isn't in the kitchen –

ISABELLE.

Or the hall –

LISETTE.

I'll bet he's up here.

ERASTE.

Maybe we should call.

ISABELLE.

Monsieur Geronte?

CRISPIN.

MONSIEUR GERONTE!

LISETTE.

You frog!

ERASTE.

Where are you, uncle?

CRISPIN.

Are you there?

LISETTE.

Warthog!

I'd like to throw his carcass in the ashbox!

GERONTE.

(Calling from upstairs, offstage.)

Lisette, Crispin! Eraste! Aaarrrggghhh!

*(**LISETTE** flings open a door on the balcony just as he comes barreling through it in his wheelchair, hits the balcony rail, and goes sailing over it, flying out of the wheelchair and landing below, behind the couch. The trick is done, of course, with a dummy. The real **GERONTE** is already positioned behind the couch, bandaged for the next scene. The four watch the catastrophe in stunned silence. There is a pause, then the head of **GERONTE** appears from behind the couch. He croaks:)*

Where's my cashbox?!

(His head disappears back behind the sofa, and the lights go to black.)

Scene Two

(When the lights come up again, after a short musical interlude, GERONTE is in his wheelchair, bandaged from head to toe and still alive. Two GENDARMES (regular size) are looking around the room for clues. CRISPIN and LISETTE do their asides as the GENDARMES finish up their investigation and prepare to ask questions. ERASTE and ISABELLE are standing together, ISABELLE next to a chair.)

CRISPIN.

I thought you'd said that he was dead.

LISETTE.

He was.

CRISPIN.

He looks good for a dead man.

LISETTE.

Yes, he does.

Well?

CRISPIN.

Well? Well what?

LISETTE.

What are we going to do?

CRISPIN.

Wait for the perfect pathway to pursue.
Stay calm, my pigeon, that's the strategy.

(Aside.)

Sweet are the uses of adversity.

GENDARME.

Your name, monsieur?

GERONTE.

Geronte.

GENDARME.

(To **ASSISTANT.***)*

Geronte.

ASSISTANT.

(Writing.)

Geronte.

GENDARME.

Your address?

GERONTE.

Twenty-two, Rue de la Fonte.

ASSISTANT.

(Stopping **GENDARME** *before he can say it.)*

I heard.

GENDARME.

Now tell us please, all the events
Preceding the attack.

GERONTE.

Well, to commence,
I spent a frightful night.

GENDARME.

(To **ASSISTANT.***)*

A frightful night.

ASSISTANT.

I HEARD!

GERONTE.

Today I had no appetite.

GENDARME.

Aha!

ASSISTANT.

Aha?

GERONTE.

My nephew broke a vase... *[vahz]*

GENDARME & ASSISTANT.

Aha!

GERONTE.

Two cousins came, two rude bourgeois.

They threatened me, they tortured me!

GENDARME & ASSISTANT.

Aha!

GERONTE.

That girl came over too, with her mamá.

GENDARME.

The names?

ERASTE.

Madame Argante and Isabelle.

GENDARME.

Suspicious.

ASSISTANT.

Yes.

CRISPIN.

Monsieur, let me dispel

Such thoughts at once. The lady could not be

Involved in this bizarre calamity.

GENDARME.

Make note of that.

ASSISTANT.

The girl and her mamá…

ERASTE.

That's right, she doesn't know a thing.

GENDARME & ASSISTANT.

Aha!

GENDARME.

And who is this young man?

GERONTE.

My nephew.

ASSISTANT.

                                                    Oh?

GENDARME.

Tell us, monsieur, exactly what you know.

ERASTE.

I –

GERONTE.

Nothing. He's a blith'ring idiot.

GENDARME.

(To **CRISPIN.***)*

And you, are you involved in this?

CRISPIN.

                              Somewhat.

ASSISTANT.

(Writing.)

Somewhat…

GENDARME.

I think you'd best elaborate.

CRISPIN.

Well, it was yesterday at two – no, wait!
It must have been today.

LISETTE.

Two days ago.

CRISPIN.

Can that be right?

LISETTE.

Of course.

CRISPIN.

You think?

LISETTE.

                              I know.

GENDARME.

(To **LISETTE.***)*

And who are you?

LISETTE.

Lisette, the maid…

ASSISTANT.

The maid…

GENDARME.

And what is your part in this escapade?

LISETTE.

If you ask me, those cousins were suspicious.

ASSISTANT.

(Rifling through the notes.)

The cousins…

GENDARME.

Ah, the cousins!

GERONTE.

They were vicious!

They brought about my latest seizure!

GENDARME & ASSISTANT.

Oh?

CRISPIN.

That's absolutely true.

LISETTE.

And he should know.

GENDARME.

We'll have that cashbox back to you bientôt.

Don't worry, the conclusion is foregone.

And now we must be –

MME ARGANTE.

(Bursting through the front door.)

What is going on!

My daughter in this madhouse! Isabelle!
Come home this moment!

ISABELLE.

No, mamá.

MME ARGANTE.

Well!

CRISPIN & LISETTE.

Well!

MME ARGANTE.

What's happened here?

LISETTE.

What hasn't?

GENDARME.

Who is she?

LISETTE.

The mother of the other one.

GENDARME.

I see.

And what do you know, madam?

MME ARGANTE.

Everything!

Good manners, piano, voice, embroidering...

GENDARME.

About the cashbox!

MME ARGANTE.

Sir! I never speak
Of money to a stranger. It's not chic.

CRISPIN.

There's been a robbery.

MME ARGANTE.

In this quartier?

Impossible! Such things are déclassé.

GENDARME.

I think we'd best be going, now, Albert. *[Albair]*

We must get back to notre commissaire.

We shall return.

ASSISTANT.

That is the protocol.

Au revoir.

    (They leave.)

CRISPIN.

Good men.

GERONTE.

No.

CRISPIN.

    No? Why not?

GERONTE.

          Too tall.

But where's my cashbox?

ISABELLE.

I don't know.

MME ARGANTE.

     Nor I.

LISETTE.

Don't look at me.

CRISPIN.

A plot to mystify.

GERONTE.

Did anyone hear noises?

LISETTE.

No.

CRISPIN.

    No.

ERASTE.

     No.

GERONTE.

Did anyone see someone come or go?

LISETTE.

Perhaps –

ERASTE.

I think –

ISABELLE.

It might be –

CRISPIN.

No.

LISETTE.

No.

ERASTE.

No.

LISETTE.

You see, sir, we were with you all the time!

CRISPIN.

(Getting an idea.)

The perfect moment to commit a crime!
The thief sneaks in a window, looks around,
He listens…

LISETTE.

But there's not a single sound.

CRISPIN.

Then, suddenly, from up above he hears –

LISETTE.

A dreadful, rattling gasp to pierce the ears!

CRISPIN.

That's you sir, as you lay upon your bed.

LISETTE.

We heard that gasp and thought that you were dead.

CRISPIN.

And so we all came down to mourn and cry.

(They begin crying.)

LISETTE.

We wailed, "Oh God! Why did he have to die?"

GERONTE.

You did?

CRISPIN.

We did.

ERASTE.

We did? I mean we did!

CRISPIN.

The brigand thief had found a spot and hid,
Then while we mourned he must have gone in there
To do the deed while we were unaware,
Lamenting your demise.

GERONTE.

Lamenting?

LISETTE.

Yes.

It was a dreadful blow, I must confess.

GERONTE.

A blow?

ERASTE.

Oh Uncle, I –

GERONTE.

(Snapping.)

What is it?!

ERASTE.

I...

(He can't do it. He turns to **CRISPIN***, aside.)*

Please tell him for me.

CRISPIN.

No, you've got to try!

*(***ERASTE** *starts to give him the look.)*

CRISPIN.

All right!

(To **GERONTE.***)*

Monsieur, your nephew –

(The doorbell rings.)

GERONTE.

There's the bell.

LISETTE.

The lawyers.

CRISPIN.

With the will.

CRISPIN & ERASTE.

(To their sweethearts.)

Adieu.

LISETTE & ISABELLE.

Farewell!

*(***LISETTE*** opens the door and motions them to come in.)*

NOTARY.

Monsieur! You're looking better, I confess,
Since last we saw you –

CRISPIN.

(Interrupting and throwing him into a chair.)

Sit down!

LISETTE.

(Aside to **CRISPIN.***)*

What a mess.

GERONTE.

I'm looking better?

NOTARY.

Yes! In just one hour

Or less you have recovered! What a power
The writing of a will can give.

GERONTE.

How true.

LISETTE.

Oh here it comes.

ERASTE.

We're lost.

CRISPIN.

Tout est perdu.

NOTARY.

And here it is!

GERONTE.

Oh, thank you! Here is what?

NOTARY.

Your will.

GERONTE.

Made out already?

NOTARY.

You forgot?

CRISPIN.

(Aside.)

Aha! That's it! Here comes the counterplot.

GERONTE.

But I called you to draw my will for me!

NOTARY.

Indeed you did and here it is.

GERONTE.

I see!

But how did you know what to write?

NOTARY.

You made

Your wishes very clear.

GERONTE.

And you were paid?

NOTARY.

Not yet, monsieur.

GERONTE.

I must have done it then.

NOTARY.

You have my word, sir, as a gentleman.

Those three were there, monsieur, they'll tell you so.

GERONTE.

Lisette!

LISETTE.

Yes, dearest master?

(Aside.)

Here I go.

GERONTE.

Well? What have you to say?

LISETTE.

I cannot speak,

I'm choked with tears.

ERASTE.

And I.

ISABELLE.

My knees are weak.

GERONTE.

What happened here?

CRISPIN.

Within this very room,

An old man sat there in the shadow's gloom,

His shawl tucked 'round his shoulders and his cap

Upon his head, a blanket in his lap –

GERONTE.

It sounds like me –

CRISPIN.

Indeed, sir, yes it does.

ERASTE.

It must have been.

ISABELLE.

Oh yes!

LISETTE.

I'd say it was.

GERONTE.

But I do not remember it –

CRISPIN.

Perchance

It could be, sir, that you were in a trance.

LISETTE.

(Picking up on the ruse immediately, turning to the **NOTARY.***)*

He's having scizures regularly.

ASSISTANT.

Oh?

LISETTE.

Do you remember several hours ago
The ladies came to visit?

GERONTE.

That I do.

LISETTE.

And then two cousins came to visit you?

GERONTE.

Don't mention them!

LISETTE.

Right. After they had gone
You fell into a stupor thereupon,

Were taken to your room...

CRISPIN.

Oh sad mischance...

LISETTE.

And quite abruptly fell into a trance.

CRISPIN.

Then, after several hours of mournful grieving,
You sighed, you turned your head and said, "I'm leaving."

LISETTE.

We thought that you had...gone –

GERONTE.

I don't recall.

CRISPIN.

Heartbroken, we came out into the hall...

LISETTE.

No sadder group than we in all of France...

CRISPIN.

How could we know that you were –

CRISPIN, LISETTE, ISABELLE & ERASTE.

In a trance?

GERONTE.

Unconscious then, I'm now led to assume,
I came downstairs into this living room,
An old man, stalked by death and indigent,
To give my final will and testament,
Discussing legal matters and finance,
Dictating it while I was in a trance?

CRISPIN.

That's right.

LISETTE.

Sounds good.

ERASTE.

Makes sense.

ISABELLE.

I'm sure it's so.

GERONTE.

What did I say in it, I'd like to know?

CRISPIN.

What did he say?

GERONTE.

Who is my legatee?

(Reading.)

To him who's been a son to me –

(To **ERASTE.***)*

YOU?

ERASTE.

Me.

GERONTE.

Impossible!

(Reading again.)

Plus an annuity

To whom?

(He is struggling to read the name.)

ASSISTANT.

It looks like Crispin at a glance.

GERONTE.

Crispin! You mean I left –

CRISPIN & LISETTE.

It was your trance.

NOTARY.

You did say so, monsieur.

GERONTE.

Remarkable!

A yearly wage to you? That's pitiful!

There's something odd occurring in this manse.

I'll find out what's the matter!

LISETTE, CRISPIN & ERASTE.

It's your trance.

GERONTE.

(Reading again.)

Two thousand crowns – a gift in cash – to you?!
"My dear Lisette, who stood me well in lieu
Of servant, nurse, companion, dearest friend!"
How I said that I cannot comprehend.

(He continues to read to himself. **CRISPIN** *and*
LISETTE *speak aside.)*

LISETTE.

We've been through intrigue, artifice and theft.

CRISPIN.

I haven't any more disguises left!

LISETTE.

The game is up.

CRISPIN.

Not necessarily.
There still remains one final strategy.

LISETTE.

What is it?

CRISPIN.

Stem your curiosity.
It just may work, or it may not – we'll see.

GERONTE.

I'll change my will again!

CRISPIN.

(Rushing to the study door.)

What's that I hear?!
Ssh! Someone's in there! Someone bad, I fear!

(Peeking in the door.)

The robber!

ISABELLE & MME ARGANTE.

Oh!

CRISPIN.

He's got the cashbox! And,
He's rifling through your desk!

LISETTE.

(*Aside to* **CRISPIN.**)

What have you planned?

MME ARGANTE.

Oh dear, what shall we do?

GERONTE.

Yes, what indeed?

CRISPIN.

One thing for certain, we must act with speed.

(*He grabs* **ERASTE** *and pulls him toward the door.*)

It's you and I –

ERASTE.

I beg your pardon?

CRISPIN.

We

Will go in there and set that cashbox free.

ERASTE.

We will?

CRISPIN.

(*Aside to him.*)

Leave everything to me, my friend.

(*Hands him a sword from the wall.*)

Believe me, you'll be able to defend
Yourself, your uncle, Isabelle, madame,
Lisette and me.

ERASTE.

I will?

CRISPIN.

(*To* EVERYONE.)

How proud I am!
Your nephew, sir, whom you think a buffoon
Will soon have pieces of this brigand strewn
About the study.

(*To* ERASTE.)

Go!

ERASTE.

In there?

CRISPIN.

At once!

(*Aside.*)

And this will be the best of all my stunts.

(*He pushes* ERASTE *into the study. There is a pause.*)

MME ARGANTE.

I can't stand the suspense!

GERONTE.

What's happening?

ISABELLE.

It's very quiet.

LISETTE.

I can't hear a thing.

(*They all lean in slightly toward the study door. [Note: The screen from Act I has been placed so that* ERASTE *can emerge from the study and talk to* CRISPIN *without being seen by the other actors.]* ERASTE *emerges.*)

CRISPIN.

Mon capitaine!

ERASTE.

(Whispering.)

There's no one in there.

CRISPIN.

(Loudly.)

Brute!

ERASTE.

(Thinking he is the brute.)

Who, me?

CRISPIN.

(Ripping the sleeve of **ERASTE**'s *jacket.)*

Take that, you dog!

ERASTE.

You ripped my suit!

CRISPIN.

(Whispering to **ERASTE**.)

Get back into that room!

ERASTE.

There's no one there!

CRISPIN.

(To **ERASTE**.)

Get me the sword from off the wall.

(To the others.)

Beware!

The thief has drawn his sword!

MME ARGANTE.

What shall we do?!

*(***ERASTE** comes back with a sword for **CRISPIN**.)*

ERASTE.

But I don't –

CRISPIN.

Trust me. I know what to do.

(To the others.)

Oh no! The study door's thrown open wide!

They're coming in here! Everybody, hide!

> *(**LISETTE** throws a shawl over **GERONTE**'s head.*
> ***MME ARGANTE** goes right under the table. The*
> ***NOTARIES** hide behind a curtain. **ISABELLE** drops*
> *behind a chair. **CRISPIN** motions to **ERASTE**, who*
> *emerges from the study.)*

> *(Whispering to him.)*

Say this, "Take that you swine!"

ERASTE.

(Whispering.)

Take that, you swine.

CRISPIN.

No, loud!

> *(He pokes him with his sword.)*

ERASTE.

"Take that, you swine!!" But why –

CRISPIN.

That's fine.

Now make some noise.

> *(They turn over a chair.)*

Aha!

NOTARY.

What are they doing?

GERONTE.

What's going on out there?

CRISPIN.

He is pursuing

The brigand thief about the room –

ISABELLE.

Oh dear!

CRISPIN.

(To **ERASTE.***)*

Attack!

(To the others, as **ERASTE** *makes a feeble attempt.)*

They're dueling!

ALL.

Oh!

CRISPIN.

A musketeer

He is!

GERONTE.

Eraste?

CRISPIN.

Indeed! Such bravery!

He's fallen! Now he fights him on one knee!

GERONTE.

Eraste?

CRISPIN.

The same! He's dropped his sword!

ALL.

Which one?

CRISPIN.

The thief!

ALL.

(Relieved.)

Oh!

CRISPIN.

Now he strikes him!

ERASTE.

(Receiving a punch in the eye from **CRISPIN.***)*

Ow!

CRISPIN.

(Aside to **ERASTE***.)*

Well done!

(He pulls **ERASTE***'s sword belt off, musses his hair, dirties his face from a potted plant, turns furniture over, etc.)*

Aha! The final reckoning! He fights
The filcher fist-to-fist! He kicks, he bites!

(He smacks his fist into his own hand, **ERASTE** *does the same.)*

ALL.

The filcher?

CRISPIN.

Yes, of course. The final blow!
But wait – the rifler strikes again!

ISABELLE.

Oh no!

CRISPIN.

They're moving back into the study now...
The spoiler tries to run – oh what a row!
Eraste springs up, and pins him to the floor –
A thrust of sword...the blackguard is no more.

(Pulling a disheveled **ERASTE***, who is already sporting a black eye, from the study.)*

It's safe. You may emerge now. It's all done.
The fight is over and the battle's won.

GERONTE.

Astounding!

MME ARGANTE.

Splendid!

ISABELLE.

Rapture!

LISETTE.

What a man!

CRISPIN.

The victor!

GERONTE.

Nephew!

ISABELLE.

Darling!

LISETTE.

(Aside to CRISPIN.)

Clever plan.

GERONTE.

But where's my cashbox?

CRISPIN.

Cashbox? …It's in there.

(Pointing to the study and going to LISETTE, aside.)

Where is it?

LISETTE.

(Pointing to ERASTE.)

I gave it to him!

CRISPIN.

(Aside to ERASTE.)

And where

Did you deposit it?

ERASTE.

With Isabelle!

CRISPIN.

(Aside to ISABELLE.)

And do you have it?

ISABELLE.

Yes, indeed.

(She lifts her skirt daintily and reveals the cashbox between her shapely calves.)

CRISPIN.

Well, well!

(During the next lines he inches **ISABELLE***, who must hop with the cashbox between her feet, to the study door.* **CRISPIN** *whisks it out from under her skirt and gives it to* **GERONTE***.)*

Good sir, your fortune is restored to you.

But fortune is much more than revenue.

It numbers love and kindness, friendship, trust.

A man without these lives in ash and dust.

Yet here within this house these riches dwell

Which you, monsieur, seem eager to dispel

For what good cause? To turn away a love

That comes to you on wings from Heav'n above?

A brother who esteemed you well and long,

Sends you his only child to right his wrong.

A lad, full-grown to manhood, knowing only

Love by you rebuked. Unwanted, lonely,

He prays for you to greet his love before

The death knell tolls and you exist no more.

His very life would he lay down for you

To hear a kind word, 'ere you bid adieu.

(All are weeping. **GERONTE** *sits there, not moving. Finally the sniffles die down, and they all stand, looking at him.)*

GERONTE.

Eraste!

ERASTE.

Yes, sir?

GERONTE.

Come here.

ERASTE.

(He goes.)

Sir?

GERONTE.

Is that true?

ERASTE.

Yes, Uncle.

GERONTE.

Well, there's nothing left to do.

(To **NOTARY.***)*

You!

NOTARY.

Yes, monsieur?

GERONTE.

Come here.

(He goes.)

This will I wrote?

NOTARY.

Yes, sir?

GERONTE.

It's valid.

LISETTE.

Why, you sweet old goat!

GERONTE.

Shut up, you tart!

LISETTE.

Old crab!

GERONTE.

You menial!

CRISPIN.

(Pulling **LISETTE** *aside.)*

We're in the will...let's be congenial!

CRISPIN.

(To **GERONTE.** *)*

Good master, to us all you have redeemed
Your troubled, agéd soul which long has seemed
To shun the greater joys that God bestows.
In perfect peace your heart can now repose,
Which, given and returned will 'eer abound,
Content in the affection you have found.
As my old friend the Cardinal said one night,
"To love and be belov'd is God's great glory!"
Ah Dieu! Those days –

ALL.

But that's another story.

CRISPIN.

Lisette, let's have a toast! Get some champagne!

GERONTE.

My heart!

CRISPIN.

That's happiness.

GERONTE.

No, it's a pain!
Death lays its icy hand upon my brow –
Yes, yes, my rendez-vous with death is now!

LISETTE.

Well, that's your third encounter for today.

GERONTE.

Virago!

LISETTE.

Dragon!

GERONTE.

(Seeing a vision.)

Ah, the chevalier
Arrives to take my hand and lead me on...

Goodbye, my boy –

ERASTE.

Oh, uncle!

GERONTE.

I...am...gone.

(There is a long pause. Everyone watches him to see if he stirs. He doesn't. **LISETTE** *listens to his chest with her ear and shakes her head.* **CRISPIN** *lifts the old man's wrist and lets it drop.)*

CRISPIN.

Eraste –

ERASTE.

Don't say it! Words to fill with dread!

CRISPIN.

My boy, your uncle's fallen cold and dead.

Dead for a ducat.

MME ARGANTE.

How untimely!

CRISPIN.

No.

Death keeps no cal'nder.

LISETTE.

When you go, you go.

ISABELLE.

Oh, poor monsieur!

CRISPIN.

All dead and turned to clay.

ERASTE.

Ah, sadness comes to visit us today.

MME ARGANTE.

But sweet is death that puts an end to pain.

NOTARY.

He's resting in the Heavenly domain.

CRISPIN.

Where all is peaceful –

ERASTE.

Tranquil –

NOTARY.

Quiet –

ASSISTANT.

Still.

ISABELLE.

Ah, me.

MME ARGANTE.

When is the reading of the will?

CRISPIN.

Tomorrow ten o'clock.

MME ARGANTE.

We'll be there.

LISETTE.

Good.

ERASTE.

We ought to get the doctors.

CRISPIN.

Yes, we should.

ISABELLE.

I'll put his head upon this little pillow.

CRISPIN.

Let's leave him now.

(*Everyone slowly backs out of the room.* **LISETTE** *is last; just before she exits, she comes back and kicks the old man to make sure he's really dead. He doesn't move. She walks to her exit, turns, and says:*)

LISETTE.

Rhinoc'ros!

(She leaves. All is very still for a long moment. Suddenly, **GERONTE** *sits up and barks:)*

GERONTE.

Armadillo!

(And laughs gleefully as the lights pin out on him.)

CURTAIN CALLS & EPILOGUE

(When the lights come up again the two **NOTARIES/ GENDARMES** *enter, one as the* **NOTARY** *and the other as the* **GENDARME**. *They bow, exchange hats, and bow again, then they escort* **MME ARGANTE** *in. She bows, then* **ISABELLE** *and* **ERASTE**; *she bows first, then he, then* **LISETTE** *and* **CRISPIN**, *the latter taking the last bow. They do a company bow and in the middle of it, remember* **GERONTE**, *who is still lying dead behind them. They part in the middle, turn their heads away from him in respect. He sits up and bows, then falls back as the cast looks back at him.* **CRISPIN** *steps forward with a piece of paper to deliver the epilogue, but* **ISABELLE** *grabs the paper from him.)*

ISABELLE.

Now just a minute! All who did this play
Have had a pretty peck of words to say,
Except for me. Not even one small speech!
So please forgive me for this awkward breach
Of manners, but I mean to have my say,
And speak the final passage of this play.

(She reads from the paper.)

Good ladies, gentlemen, to well present
The mask of comedy was our intent.
And if, perchance, a feeling pierced your soul,
Inspired by this modest...

(She asks **CRISPIN** *about the upcoming word.)*

barcarole,
Then we have labored well, for what's a play?

A flow'ring of our thought, a sweet bouquet
Of sights and sighs and sounds, all joys and woes
Enwoven in mercurial tableaux.
A lucent crystal mirror to this plane.
But in this purpose here to entertain
We are no more than silence gone unheard
Without the listening ear to hear the word
And cheer the effort here within this hall,

> *(She acknowledges the audience.)*

And so to you – great players one and all!

> *(The actors applaud **ISABELLE**, then they all applaud the audience.)*

End of Play